MEET THE

Fortune of the [...]
(Shh! Nobody kn[...])

Age: 25

Vital Statistics: The sexy Frenchman has blue eyes, tousled brown hair and that certain je ne sais quoi.

Claim to Fame: He is a renowned winemaker, a brash blogger and the toast of Paris.

Romantic Prospects: His reputation with the ladies is legendary. Just don't ask him for a commitment.

"Nothing has gone according to plan since I arrived in Austin. When Kate Fortune asked me here to consult on a business venture, I figured I would be in and out in twenty-four hours. But I hadn't counted on Robin, Kate's landscape gardener. From the moment I saw her, I was... *enchanté.*

"Robin would never believe that Paris's enfant terrible is actually one of Jerome Fortune's bastard children. And as far as I am concerned, she does not need to know. Up next: a brief but dazzling affaire de coeur. By the time Christmas comes, I will be far across the sea. But can I romance fair Robin and then leave her behind?"

THE FORTUNES OF TEXAS

Dear Reader,

Welcome to Texas! And to my latest book from Harlequin Special Edition, *A Fortunes of Texas Christmas*.

I'm delighted to have the opportunity to write for The Fortunes of Texas continuity and to introduce you to another of Gerald Robinson's—aka Jerome Fortune's—secret children, Amersen Beaudin. He's young, successful, brash and deliciously French! He's in Austin, Texas, for business, but can't deny who he is and the family he isn't sure he wants to know. And he's *always* used to getting his own way. Until he meets Robin, a hardworking, down-to-earth girl with a heart as big as Texas and the gumption to match his! Of course, the road to love is never easy—what would be the fun in that?

Thank you for taking the time to read *A Fortunes of Texas Christmas*. I truly hope you enjoy Amersen and Robin's story.

I adore hearing from readers and can be reached by email at mail@helenlacey.com, on Twitter, @helen_lacey_, and on Facebook, or sign up for my newsletter via my website at helenlacey.com. Please visit anytime as I love talking about my pets, my horses and, of course, cowboys and also sharing news about upcoming books in my latest series for Harlequin Special Edition, The Cedar River Cowboys!

Warmest holiday wishes,

Helen Lacey

A Fortunes of Texas Christmas

Helen Lacey

HARLEQUIN® SPECIAL EDITION®

Special thanks and acknowledgment are given to Helen Lacey for her contribution to The Fortunes of Texas continuity.

Recycling programs
for this product may
not exist in your area.

ISBN-13: 978-0-373-62390-7

A Fortunes of Texas Christmas

Printed in U.S.A.

www.Harlequin.com

Helen Lacey grew up reading *Black Beauty* and *Little House on the Prairie*. These childhood classics inspired her to write her first book when she was seven, a story about a girl and her horse. She loves writing for Harlequin Special Edition, where she can create strong heroes with soft hearts and heroines with gumption who get their happily-ever-after. For more about Helen, visit her website, helenlacey.com.

Books by Helen Lacey

Harlequin Special Edition

The Cedar River Cowboys

The Rancher's Unexpected Family
Married to the Mom-to-Be
The Cowgirl's Forever Family
Lucy & the Lieutenant
Three Reasons to Wed

The Prestons of Crystal Point

The CEO's Baby Surprise

Claiming His Brother's Baby
Once Upon a Bride
Date with Destiny
His-and-Hers Family
Marriage Under the Mistletoe
Made for Marriage

Visit the Author Profile page
at Harlequin.com for more titles.

For Dawn and Ray.
Good neighbors, great friends.

Chapter One

Amersen Beaudin hated flying.

Despite the fact that he'd racked up more frequent-flyer miles in the past five years than most people did in a lifetime, not even the luxurious private jet he was currently seated in was enough to change his opinion. Still, he thought as he stretched out his legs and sipped on a twenty-five-year-old scotch, this was definitely better than traveling coach. Not that he'd done that for several years. He closed his eyes and thought about what he was about to walk into once he landed in Austin.

Fortunes.

More than he'd ever wanted to meet. Or know.

But ninetysomething matriarch and business icon Kate Fortune had requested his presence, and she wasn't an easy woman to refuse. And plus, he was curious. Despite everything. Despite knowing he was opening the book on the past. And despite recently finding out he had Fortune blood coursing through his veins. But since he had no intention of ever accepting the notion that he was a *Fortune*, Amersen figured he'd meet with Kate, listen to what she had to say and then decide if he wanted any more involvement with Texas, with Austin or with anyone named Fortune.

Kate's call a couple of weeks earlier had come from

left field. A business proposition, she'd said. Something that was worth discussing in person and not over the telephone. And no mention of anything personal. No mention of the fact that he was Jerome Fortune's—aka Gerald Robinson's—son. *Illegitimate son.* But not really his son, since Amersen did not consider Gerald Robinson to be his father. He had a father, and a damned good one, back in Paris. Nothing would change that. Not the notion that he was actually one of several children sired and abandoned by computer giant Gerald Robinson—a man who'd faked his own death years earlier and had been outed as the philandering Jerome Fortune less than two years ago. Blood didn't make someone a parent. Love and commitment did. And Amersen had that back in Paris. With his mother, Suzette, his stepfather, Luc Beaudin, and his younger sister, Claire, he had all the family he needed.

This trip was merely out of curiosity and respect. Kate Fortune was a highly successful woman, and even though she was no longer the CEO, she was still considered the powerhouse behind Fortune Cosmetics and many other business ventures. And since Kate hadn't mentioned anything about him being Gerald's son, Amersen suspected her request for a meeting was about something else altogether.

At least, that was what he hoped. It had been hard enough ignoring emails and shutting down telephone calls from two of his half brothers over the past few months. Keaton Fortune Whitfield and Ben Fortune Robinson had made it clear they wanted to meet him, but Amersen had held back. Finding out he was Gerald Robinson/Jerome Fortune's unwanted son was one thing. Embracing the knowledge he had enough siblings to form a soccer team was something else. Gerald had eight children from his long marriage to Charlotte Prendergast Robinson, plus several out of wedlock with other women, including his mother, who had been the au pair to the Fortune children twenty-six years ago. Which made Gerald a womanizing, cheating, no-good bastard.

And definitely not someone Amersen wanted in his life.

That decided, he'd meet with Kate Fortune, listen to her proposition and then head straight back to Paris, where he belonged. With any luck, Keaton Fortune Whitfield and Ben Fortune Robinson wouldn't even know he'd touched down on their turf. Maybe he'd meet them one day. But not now. He didn't want anything derailing his life.

The last few years had been good ones, during which he'd worked tirelessly to achieve all that he had. The blog he'd started in college, called *The Real Paris*, had earned him something of a celebrity status, along with some notoriety and labels such as opinionated, ruthless and arrogant. But he could live with the labels. He was grateful for the trajectory it had taken him on and the opportunities it offered in its wake. Like Noir, the nightclub he'd built from the ground up in an abandoned warehouse in the heart of the city over five years earlier, when he was twenty. The place had taken on a life force of its own and was now frequented by the Parisian elite and countless international celebrities. Noir was upscale, high-end and definitely the place to see and be seen in Paris. It became a money machine, and he'd quickly invested the first million he'd made in a winery and was now exporting product around the globe.

Yes, life was good for Amersen Beaudin. And he wasn't about to do anything to change that.

And that included getting too involved with the Fortune family.

By the time the jet landed at Austin-Bergstrom International Airport and he was through customs, it was nearly three o'clock in the afternoon. There was a limo and driver waiting for him, compliments of Kate Fortune, and then he was on the freeway and heading to her ranch. The driver took a left off the main road, headed toward a set of gates that had a sign saying Sterling's Fortune, then turned down a long driveway. As Amersen looked out toward the pastures dotted with horses and cattle, he couldn't help but be impressed. As far as homes went, this one looked as though it belonged on the front page of a lifestyles-of-the-rich-and-famous magazine. And probably had, he figured, considering who Kate Fortune was.

The limo pulled up outside the large house, and he got out before the driver had a chance to come around to the back of the vehicle. He was used to limos and flagrant displays of wealth but still liked to do things his own way. Sure, he was rich. And in his own country he had established a reputation and racked up a considerable bank balance and real estate portfolio. But he drove his own car and tied his own shoes.

He shrugged off all thoughts of Paris for the moment and told the driver to wait for him so he could take the car back to his hotel downtown when his meeting with Kate Fortune was over. The driver agreed, and Amersen quickly headed up the pathway toward the front door.

And then he saw her.

A vision.

A dream.

A woman so enchanting he actually blinked a couple of times to make sure he wasn't seeing things. She was walking across the garden, wearing a long white dress that seemed to float over her curves, with long sleeves that exposed her shoulders, the kind of dress that made him foolishly think of hand holding, or lounging on the grass at a picnic. He couldn't see her face as she wore a wide-brimmed, floppy white hat. But he saw her hair. It cascaded down her back in a beautiful honey-blond wave. His palms suddenly itched with the longing to feel her hair between his fingers, to wrap a fistful of her lustrous waves around his hand and draw her close. He tried to shake the idea off and failed. He tried to drag his gaze away and failed there, too.

Être toujours mon cœur...

There was something about the way she walked that rooted him to the spot, something about the tilt of her head and the sway of her hips that was impossible to ignore, and the image was suddenly imprinted in his brain like a stamp. It was illogical and foolish. He didn't get shuttled into la-la land by a pair of great hips and blond hair. Not ever. He had beautiful women in his life and in his bed whenever he wanted them. But he kept it casual. Amersen didn't have time to get bogged down in a serious relationship. He was twenty-five years old, way too young to think of commitment to any one woman.

What he didn't want, what he would never allow of himself, was to be derailed by the image of a beautiful woman in a white dress, no matter how enchanting she was. Still, he couldn't help the way his body took notice of her as she made her way across the garden and toward the small rotunda. She looked as though she belonged in a painting in the Musée d'Orsay. Or by his side, drinking champagne on a balcony overlooking the Seine.

He cursed himself for being so stupidly sentimental.

But he couldn't help how his palms itched. Or how his blood heated and seemed to unexpectedly surge to one part of his anatomy. He could usually control attraction. But this…this was like a lightning strike, as though every breath he inhaled was somehow being sucked out through his skin, and suddenly he couldn't get enough air into his lungs. A familiar dread crept into his limbs as his throat tightened. Sweat broke out on the back of his neck when he realized what was coming.

Damn. The last thing he wanted to do was have an asthma attack on Kate Fortune's lawn. Amersen cursed his weak lungs for the trillionth time and straightened his back, rounding out his shoulders, slowing down his breathing as much as he could. He hadn't had a full-blown attack for months and couldn't believe he was suddenly at risk because he'd spotted a goddess in white walking across the garden. His attention wasn't usually so easily distracted. He needed to get himself under control…and fast.

Amersen took a breath, and then another, forcing air into his body, trying to relax his constricting lungs the old-fashioned way, reluctant to use the inhaler in his pocket. He took another breath, and then another, until finally he felt his lungs relax and the air began to flow through his nose and down his throat, and he began to feel normal again. He glanced toward the house and then diverted his gaze back to the woman still walking across the garden.

He willed his legs to turn, to move, to make for the house so he could get himself back under control. But he stayed where he was, watching as she walked around the rotunda, her face hidden, her hips swaying. And then, almost as though she had been an apparition, she was gone.

Before he could stop himself, Amersen was hiking toward the rotunda and darting up the steps two at a time, looking for her, suddenly desperate to talk to her. But, nothing. There was a small set of stairs opposite the ones he'd climbed, and he stood on the top step and looked around. Still nothing. Amersen rubbed his eyes wearily. Maybe jet lag had settled in and he'd imagined her. Maybe he was losing his mind.

"Can I help you?"

He stilled, rooted to the spot for a moment before he slowly turned on his heels. She was behind him, and he stared at her, wishing he could see all of her face beneath the brim of that hat. He got a glimpse of her chin and her luscious pink mouth and the slant of her cheeks, but it was her eyes he was suddenly desperate for. He wanted the visual connection, that first look that was a prelude to everything else. And her soft Texas drawl was unexpectedly a complete turn-on.

"I don't know," he said quietly, his pulse quickening. "Can you?"

Robin Harbin stared at the man in front of her, her belly dipping wildly, like she was on a theme park roller coaster going way too fast. But, boy, the man was gorgeous. Maybe the most perfectly handsome male specimen she'd ever seen. Black hair, riveting blue eyes, a strong jaw just touched with a shadow of whiskers... and a body that quickly sent her libido—and her traitorous ovaries—into serious overdrive.

Of course she knew who he was.

Amersen Beaudin.

Her employer, Kate Fortune, had mentioned him several times over the past week. A Frenchman. Someone Kate wanted to work with. And Robin's interest had been piqued enough that she had done an internet search to find out what all the fuss was about. A couple of clicks of the mouse and she had all the intel she needed. Rich, successful and a well-documented heartless playboy. Known simply as *Amersen* to his trillions of followers on social media. Okay, so maybe *trillions* was an exaggeration…but he certainly had a lot of people wanting to hear his opinion on pretty much *everything*. Robin had read a few of his blog posts and had quickly formed the view that he was an overopinionated, egotistical know-it-all who, based on what she'd seen in a few videos he'd posted, clearly loved to hear the sound of his own voice. And of course, he was totally and categorically out of her league. Not that she had any thoughts about the man in that way. She didn't know him.

But he was gorgeous.

And obviously knew it, from the way he was looking at her. As though he knew exactly what she was thinking. Irritation suddenly chugged through her veins and she dropped her chin a fraction, realizing he probably had women falling at his feet across the globe and that was why he was regarding her as though she *should* be looking at him like he was some kind of great prize. Which, she supposed, he was, but she certainly wasn't going to let him think she believed that.

"Nice…dress," he said, his lovely accent winding up her spine like liquid silk.

Robin glanced down at the white frock she'd donned half an hour earlier at Kate's request. The gown and hat were a trial look for a new brand campaign, which found Robin being photographed in the rotunda when the usual model had called in sick earlier that afternoon. Not that she considered herself model material. She was a touch too full in the bust and too curvy in the hips for that. But Kate wanted some shots to send the marketing department at Fortune Cosmetics, and Robin was the only option at the time. The truth be told, she felt a little ridiculous in the ultrafeminine dress—jeans and cowboy boots were more her style. But Kate was her employer *and* friend, and she had no intention of disappointing the older woman.

"Thank you," she said quietly, eager to get away from his burning gaze. Sheesh, the guy had the intensity thing down pat. "You're here to see Kate," she said, more statement than question.

He nodded. "Yes. Are you a relative?"

His English was perfect, and his accent was so incredibly sexy that her knees acted treacherously and threatened to buckle beneath his warm, penetrating gaze. She wanted to run, to flee from his stare and never look back. Men like Amersen Beaudin spelled trouble... and Robin had made a decision to categorically avoid trouble after breaking up with her no-good, two-timing boyfriend eight months earlier. The next man she fell for wasn't going to look like he belonged on the cover of a fashion magazine. He was going to be the complete opposite of Louse of the Century Trey Hammond. *And the complete opposite of Amersen Beaudin, for that matter.*

"No," Robin replied, ignoring the heat smacking her cheeks. "Kate's inside," she said, figuring he'd get the hint that she wasn't interested in a conversation.

"But you're out here," he said smoothly, each word a blatant flirtation.

Robin stepped back. "She's expecting you."

"I know."

"She doesn't like to be kept waiting."

His mouth twisted in an amused grin. "She sounds

formidable. Should I ask you to accompany me? For protection?"

Robin didn't dare meet his gaze. She didn't want to look directly into his brilliant blue eyes. "You look resilient enough to handle yourself, Mr. Beaudin."

He chuckled. "You know who I am?"

"I know enough," she said and stepped back. "Kate's waiting for you in the front living room. Best get a move on."

"You're very…" His voice trailed off, as though he was searching for the right word. "Bossy."

Robin almost laughed out loud. Her two older brothers always called her that. "Thank you," she said tightly. "That's the nicest compliment I've received all day."

"In that dress," he said quietly, "I doubt it. However, if *nice* is what does it for you, I'm sure I can accommodate you, Miss…"

Robin shivered. It was a blatant flirtation. Everything about the damnable man was seductive. She ignored his angling for her name. "Oh, I see," she said and raised her chin, connecting with his gaze full on. "You're one of those men who can't help but come on to every woman you meet."

She heard him suck in a sharp breath, saw his brilliant blue eyes darken. "Every woman?" he echoed and tilted his head slightly. "No."

Robin put a hand to her chest in mock appreciation. "Then I'm flattered…but not interested."

"Really?"

He sounded shocked, and it made Robin laugh. "Really," she replied. "And right now you should be thinking about your meeting with Kate and not anything… else."

He stared at her. "Is this what's called Texas hospitality?"

"No," she said and took another step. "Simply good advice, Mr. Beaudin. Good luck with your interview."

Then she turned on her heels, headed down the steps and raced around toward the guesthouse—far away from Amersen Beaudin and his absurdly sexy blue eyes. Hoping that with a little luck, she'd never have to see him again.

Must. Not. Think. He's. Sexy.

Not ever.

But she did. Which spelled nothing but trouble.

Interview?

Amersen was still mulling that idea a couple of minutes later as a plump sixtysomething housekeeper invited him inside the big house. He ignored the idea that he'd been thoroughly and emphatically rejected by the nameless garden goddess and crossed the threshold, following the woman down the hall. It was a grand home, with a wide stairway, polished floors and stylish furnishings. The front living room was equally impressive, and it occurred to him that many people would be intimidated by the wealth and opulence. But he wasn't. Maybe he'd become overused to wealth in the past few years.

And Kate Fortune was as incredible as he'd expected—she was tall and still striking despite her years, and she regarded him with a kind of high-browed curiosity as he walked through the door and introduced himself. She was standing by the fireplace, looking elegant in a shell-pink suit with an ivory silk blouse and a thin row of pearls around her neck. Her hair was neat, her makeup impeccable and her demeanor one of style personified. Yes, Kate Fortune was every bit as imposing as he'd been led to believe. But he wasn't daunted. Far from it. Amersen was keen to talk to her and hear her out.

"It was very good of you to come all this way to meet me," she said, stretching out one long, elegant hand toward him. "I trust you had a comfortable flight?"

Amersen nodded and shook her hand. "Yes, thank you. Supplying the jet for my trip was very thoughtful of you."

She shrugged lightly and then waved a hand. "Would you prefer to converse in French?"

His curiosity deepened. "You speak French, Ms. Fortune?"

"Some," she replied. "And please, call me Kate."

He nodded. "I'm happy to speak in English."

She smiled a little and motioned for him to take a seat on one of the sofas. "Yes, well, you speak it very well. You studied business at Cambridge for several years, correct?"

Amersen's brows rose fractionally as he sat down opposite her. "You've done some homework."

"Of course," she said and shrugged lightly. "I like to know who I'm going into business with."

"Is that what we're doing?"

Her mouth rose in one corner. "Time will tell, I suppose. No doubt you're curious as to why I asked you to come here."

"Yes."

She sat back. "You've heard of Fortune Cosmetics?"

"Of course."

She nodded approvingly. "It's no secret that the business is very successful in this country, but I want to extend the reach of our products. To bring something new to the brand. A kind of European flair, for want of a better expression. And I wanted to discuss that idea with you."

Amersen frowned. "You do know that I own a night-club and a winery? I mean to say, I don't have any connection to the cosmetics business in my country."

"I know that," she replied. "But when it comes to my company, I like to approach opportunities from different angles."

Amersen linked his hands together. "I know you founded the company, but I thought that Graham Fortune Robinson was now CEO of Fortune Cosmetics."

"He is," she said. "He took on the role over a year ago, and he's doing a wonderful job."

"But?" Amersen prompted.

"But Fortune Cosmetics is still my company, and I'm working on several projects at the moment. Including this one."

"I'm a project?" he asked, biting back a grin, thinking about the garden nymph and how she'd suggested he was being interviewed and how it actually felt like he was. He was almost tempted to ask Kate who the woman in the garden was. But didn't. This was the time for business.

"Potentially," Kate replied. "I want to promote the brand into Europe, and into France in particular. I would like you to help me do that."

Stunned, Amersen straightened his back. "And how would I do that, precisely?"

"I have a few ideas."

"Why me?" he asked bluntly.

She smiled lightly. "Because I think you know the French. I think you know Europe. I think you know what people want, and without sounding condescending, I believe you can recognize a good business opportunity on a level that's rarely seen in someone so young." When he opened his mouth to speak, she raised her hand a little. "Yes, I've done my research. I know much about you. I've read your blog and I'm familiar with your accomplishments, including your financial success, and I must say, I'm impressed. You have a knack for getting right down into the core of things… and people respond to that. I particularly enjoyed the blog you did recently about society's almost insatiable appetite for celebrity gossip. And since you're something of a celebrity yourself, I imagine you were speaking from experience."

Amersen shrugged. "In general terms. If you put yourself in the public eye, gossip and innuendo almost happen organically. I have a reputation for writing the truth along with a good dose of cynicism… If I'm prepared to dish it out, I have to be prepared to take it, as well."

Kate nodded and laughed softly. "Yes, exactly. You know, you and I are a lot alike, Amersen. We're both ambitious and driven by the need to have more than just an ordinary life."

Amersen stilled, wondering if she was going to mention the family connection—if that was why she believed they shared similar traits. He'd prepared himself for her questions when he'd made the decision to fly to Texas and would certainly tell Kate the truth if she asked.

"I've lived a life that many consider glamorous and entitled," she went on to say. "A life that many have envied. But I've had to work hard for every inch of my success. Much like yourself, I suspect."

Amersen waited for her to slip Gerald Robinson's

name into the conversation, figuring she had the perfect segue. But to his surprise, she didn't. "Perhaps."

She nodded agreeably. "Which is why I believe that a Beaudin/Fortune product would be a huge success. Something that would make the consumer feel a little bit of that glamour…even if it's for only a moment."

Amersen's instincts were piqued, but he wasn't about to rush into an agreement about anything. Despite his reputation for being a little wild and impulsive, at the core he was prudent when it came to business. And he wasn't about to do anything that could damage his reputation. Or his bank account.

"What kind of product are we talking about?"

"A men's product, of course," she replied. "A fragrance…something that is innately masculine, but also aspirational."

A cologne? It seemed a huge stretch from his established nightclub and wine brand. But he was intrigued by the idea and the opportunity. "And you want to put my name on the box, is that right?"

She nodded again. "Yes."

Amersen stood straighter. "It sounds risky."

"Of course," Kate said and chuckled. "But good business is often about risk. Didn't you take a risk turning that old warehouse into a nightclub five years ago?"

"Indeed. Everyone thought I had lost my mind and that it would be a complete disaster."

Her brows rose. "And everyone was wrong. I believe in risks…in taking chances. I believe in you, and I think we could do something special with this idea."

Amersen was curious, but cautious. "I need to think about it."

"Certainly," she said and smiled knowingly. "But let's not wait too long to pull together a plan. Opportunity like this doesn't come along very often, as you are no doubt aware." She got to her feet with an elegance that defied her years. "I would like to offer you a tour of the Fortune Cosmetics headquarters in town while you are here. Of course, that's if you intend to stay in Austin for a few days?"

The same headquarters where Graham Fortune Robinson worked? Amersen wasn't sure that was such a good idea and remained noncommittal. "I have a room booked at a hotel in town. I'll think about your offer and get back to you."

"Okay, we'll speak again soon."

He was being dismissed, but he didn't mind. He had a lot to think about and needed solitude to do so. "We'll talk tomorrow," he promised.

Amersen shook Kate's hand and left. He walked from the house, glancing once toward the rotunda before he got back into the limo. He pushed the memory of the woman in the white dress from his thoughts and tried to get his mind back to business. *Fortune business.* The thing was, he wasn't sure he wanted to get into bed with the Fortunes.

With the woman in the white dress, sure.

He'd take her to bed in a microsecond.

And as the limo eased down the driveway, Amersen made a mental note to ask Kate about her the next time they met. Instinct told him they'd meet again. And he *always* trusted his instincts. They'd never failed him.

And he found it particularly ironic that being Gerald Robinson's illegitimate son might just bring him good fortune.

Chapter Two

"Want to tell me what's on your mind, chickpea?"

Robin clipped up the front of Butterfly's rug and then patted the gray mare on the neck. She glanced sideways and saw her father, Cliff, staring at her. "Nothing," she said as she left the stall and closed the stable door. "And don't you think I'm a little old to still be called that?"

Cliff chuckled. "You'll always be my little girl, no matter how old you are. That's the thing with daughters," he said and grinned. "They're way more important than sons."

"Don't let Reece and Evan hear you say that," she said and laughed, thinking of her two older brothers. "And I'm twenty-four, Dad…hardly a little girl."

He grinned again in that familiar way she loved, his mouth only partially twisting thanks to a stroke he'd suffered a couple of years earlier. "Boys aren't good for much of anything. They leave home and forget about their parents."

Robin gently met her father's gaze. "They're successful lawyers, Dad," she reminded him, thinking about how proud her parents actually were that her brothers were partners at an Austin firm. "And neither of them wanted to be ranchers."

"Just as well we have you, chickpea."

"I'm only a part-time rancher," she said and hooked the hay net onto a peg by the stable door. "But you know I'm always going to be here to help you and Mom."

"Until you get married and leave," he said and moved across the stables, using the walking stick he resented, before resting on a couple of straw bales. "Mind you, if you'd married Trey, you would've stayed here, since he owns the ranch next door."

"His *parents* own the ranch next door," she corrected. "And first, I was never engaged to Trey. Second, he's on the rodeo circuit so much I don't think he'll ever settle down."

Her father visibly winced. "Sorry, chickpea... I didn't mean to bring up old hurts."

Robin shrugged. Everyone who lived within twenty miles of the ranch knew that Robin had caught Trey Hammond, her boyfriend of two years, pants down in a hotel room with two buckle bunnies. Robin had driven to Dallas to surprise him after he'd been on the road for two weeks competing in the bull-riding events at several rodeos. But she was the one who got the big surprise.

Looking back, she couldn't believe how foolishly naive she'd been. Trey was a good-looking, charming flirt—everyone said so. She'd been warned off getting involved with him for years before they'd actually begun dating. But she hadn't listened. She'd allowed her heart to do her thinking and eventually paid a whopping price for loving him. The biggest price of her life, as it had turned out. But dwelling on their broken relationship and everything that went with it wasn't her style. She'd made a promise to herself that she would never get bogged down in grief or regret.

One day she would fall in love again. She would find a nice, sensible man she could honor and trust. Not a good-looking womanizer who couldn't keep his manhood in his jeans for longer than a couple of weeks.

She checked her watch and made a sharp sound. "Jeez, I have to get to work."

Her father was regarding her gently. "You work too hard. With everything you do around here and the hours you put in at the fancy ranch of Kate Fortune's…it's no wonder you look so tired."

She smiled at her father's words. "Thanks, Dad, love you, too."

"Don't ever doubt it," he said and smiled. "Your mom and I are very proud of you."

Her throat tightened. "I know. And I've got to run. You gonna be okay?"

"Fine," he said and waved a hand. "I can finish up here. You go."

Robin gave him a quick hug and then hightailed it back to her cabin, which was down a track through the small orchard and behind the main house her parents shared. She'd moved into the cabin when she was seventeen, citing a need for privacy in a family who loved her dearly, though they could be stifling en masse. But they'd always loved and supported her, despite her tendency to do things her own way.

She took a quick shower, dressed in jeans and a dark T-shirt, grabbed her jacket and shoved her feet into her favorite boots before she got into her truck and headed east. The drive to Sterling's Fortune took less than fifteen minutes, but she loathed being late and was pleased to see she'd pulled up outside the greenhouse at five minutes to eight.

Robin adored her job. Working for Kate Fortune was a dream come true. As the master landscaper and gardener at the ranch, she spent her day doing what she loved most. Kate was fair and supportive of all of Robin's landscaping concepts and sought her advice on plants and flowers for her own private garden. She'd landed the job a couple of years earlier after finishing technical college, when she'd been working at a nursery in Austin and was at the Fortune ranch delivering Kate's new topiaries.

She knew who Kate was, of course. Everyone knew the iconic Kate Fortune. But she was surprised how genuine and down-to-earth the other woman was. They had talked for close to an hour about the ranch and Robin's job, and the following day Kate called to offer her a position as the head groundskeeper. It was a no-brainer to accept the job—better salary, great working conditions and the opportunity to showcase her skills as a landscape designer. Working for Kate was a dream come true and Robin liked the older woman and her sweet-natured husband, Sterling Foster, immensely.

"Got a call from O'Neill's this morning," Otis said the moment she dropped her bag in the small room she used as an office in the back of the greenhouse. "They said that fancy fertilizer you wanted is back in stock."

Otis Duke, in his midseventies, had a bad leg and back, but he knew more about roses and camellias than anyone she knew. She'd known him for years, ever since she was a fifth grader, in fact. Back then he was younger and fitter and had worked as a groundskeeper for the elementary school. When he was laid off due to restructuring, he'd found it impossible to get another job because of his age. But Robin wasn't fazed and had offered him a part-time position the moment Kate hired her. Otis was her right hand and a good friend. She also had two other staff who worked a rotating schedule.

Robin dropped her keys in the bowl on her makeshift

desk and turned to face Otis. "Great, thanks. I'll head into town to pick it up later." She grabbed the clipboard hanging on a hook by the door. "We have to pull up the three flower beds around the rotunda today so we can plant them out with the pansies that arrive tomorrow. I drew a quick sketch of the design," she said and pointed to the outlines. "We can use Swiss chard here, and I thought we could try using ornamental cabbage around the edge for something a little different this year."

Otis nodded. "Good choice. You certainly have an eye for this stuff. Mrs. Fortune stands a good chance of taking a prize this year."

Robin was certain that Otis cared more about the annual prizes awarded by the local arbor society than either Kate or Sterling, but she nodded agreeably and gave him a copy of the plans. They had a busy day scheduled and needed to get started. And this time, Robin thought as she walked through the greenhouse and headed for the toolshed, she wouldn't get waylaid by any kind of dazzling Frenchman.

Of course, her dreams had been plagued by images of Amersen Beaudin and his brilliant blue eyes. And broad shoulders. And hot body. But she supposed the man couldn't help it if he was sex on legs. It was pure genetics that made him so damned attractive. And, she figured, a good slug of charm.

Just stay immune...

That should be easy. With a little luck, she'd never see him again.

That decided, Robin got started on the day's chores and, after a quick trip into town to pick up the fertilizer she'd ordered, spent the remainder of the morning working on the beds around the rotunda with Otis. She was about to get to her feet and stretch out her back when the old man moved around to the patch she was digging up and called her name.

"What?" she asked, looking up.

"You know that fancy limo that was here yesterday?" he said, both brows raised.

Her insides twitched. "Yes."

"It's back."

Amersen had spent the better part of the past sixteen or so hours thinking about Kate Fortune's proposition and what it would mean if he decided to get involved. The hotel room, as swanky and comfortable as it was, had been a little cloistering, and he'd spent some of the morning walking the streets of Austin, familiarizing himself with the place. It was a nice city, and in an odd way, its diversity reminded him of Paris.

Kate called midmorning to arrange a meeting and he agreed quickly, eager to have a more detailed conversation with her about the proposal. The opportunity to be part of the Fortune portfolio appealed to him, but it also felt like a red flag waved in front of a bull.

He wasn't ready to be outed as Gerald Robinson's biological son, especially since Gerald clearly had no interest in him. And the closer he got to anyone named Fortune, the greater the risk of that happening. But to dismiss the business potential…that could turn into career suicide. He wanted to expand his brand through Europe and into the United States, and he wasn't going to let an insignificant fact such as being Gerald's illegitimate son derail those plans.

When the limo pulled up outside the ranch house, he had all his usual resolve back with a vengeance. And yet, as he got out of the limo and walked up the path to Kate's home, he was foolishly thinking about the woman in white. She'd invaded his dreams the night before—with her beautiful hair and sassy mouth—and he wanted to see her again. He looked toward the rotunda and tried to ignore the disappointment that briefly constricted his chest.

Stay focused, Beaudin.

Kate greeted him warmly, dressed impeccably in black and white iconic Chanel.

"Thank you for coming back to see me," she said. "Coffee?"

He nodded. "Sure. So, you said you had some more detail from our discussion yesterday?"

"Yes," she replied and poured coffee for them both. Once they were both seated, she pushed a narrow gray folder across the coffee table. "Take a look."

Amersen flipped through the pages, reading quickly, scanning the proposal with interest. The outline was brief but detailed enough to pique his curiosity.

"Amersen Noir," she said and smiled, her brows arched. "It has a nice ring to it, don't you think?"

He couldn't deny her savvy. Piggybacking on the success of his nightclub made good business sense.

It was cologne. High-end and obviously expensive. And with his name on the bottle. There were stats, graphs and a mocked-up illustration of the product.

"It's an interesting concept," he said quietly. "Although, as I said yesterday, I'm not sure my name alone is enough to successfully market a new fragrance."

She smiled. "Your name *and* your image. And as with any new product, there would be an extensive brand campaign...billboards, media, advertising targeted to the customer this product would be designed for—primarily eighteen- to thirty-five-year-olds with significant disposable income. Much like yourself," she added and smiled again. "Interested?"

"Intrigued," he replied. "Conceptually, it's an attractive idea. But I'm still not convinced my...*image*, as you put it, would be enough enticement as a selling tool."

"You're being modest."

Amersen laughed. "Once you get to know me, Ms. Fortune, you'll discover that modesty isn't something I'm known for."

Her mouth curled. "I'm quite aware of your image, Amersen. And your reputation. You're successful, hard-working, arrogant, opinionated, brash *and* cynical. And that's what this product and campaign needs. I think you possess that elusive Midas touch. And I want to capitalize on that, because it's good business."

Kate was frank, which he liked, but her confidence didn't entirely allay his concerns. "And what if these arrogant, spendthrift workaholics don't come to the party?"

"They will," she assured him. "I have a sense about these things. So do you," she said pointedly. "That's why you're a millionaire many times over. And why you pour so much effort into your nightclub and your wine brand. Young men will buy this product because they want to be like you. And young women will buy this product because they want their young men to *be* you."

He raised a brow. "That's quite an endorsement."

"It's all in the proposal," she said and motioned to the folder in his hand. "We tested the market, did some core group evaluations...the results all came back positive. But if you need more, let's say, *immediate* assurance, just bear with me a moment."

She stood and walked toward the small writing desk by the fireplace. She made a quick call, fiddled with a few files on the desk and then turned back to him.

Amersen got to his feet and was about to speak when the door opened and a young woman suddenly stood at the threshold.

It was *her*.

Only this time she wasn't wearing a white dress. She wore jeans, a shirt and boots and held gardening gloves in one hand. Still, he'd never seen a more beautiful woman in his life. Her eyes were brilliantly blue, her long hair cascading down her back. And she had curves that were so damned sexy that his libido did a wild leap.

"So," Kate said, looking toward the younger woman. "What do you think?"

"What do I think?"

The sexy drawl made his blood surge.

"Of him," Kate replied, waving a hand. "First impressions. And be brutally honest."

Amersen ignored the notion that he was suddenly about to be studied like something under a microscope. His ego was healthy enough to take a little visual assessment. Plus, it gave him time to look her over in return. And he did look. Every second stretched like elastic. She didn't say a word; she simply let her eyes roll over him, up and down, and he did the same, missing nothing, lingering in places that in other circumstances might be considered highly inappropriate.

When his gaze returned to her face, she was waiting for him, and the connection was so hot it was visceral. He didn't imagine how her mouth parted fractionally, or how her cheeks were now tinged with color. But she didn't back down. She met him stare for stare. She had gumption by the bucket load, and he suddenly discovered that he liked gumption…a lot.

Finally, she spoke. "Ms. Fortune, this man is hot."

Amersen bit back his amusement at her outrageous re-

sponse. Because he *was* hot…right under the collar. And
she knew it! There was flirtation in her dancing blue eyes.
And awareness. And mischief. He knew those things well.
They were usually his trademark when confronted by an
attractive woman. Only now, with this woman, he felt as
though the tables had been well and truly turned.

"Amersen, this is Robin Harbin," Kate said. "She's the
master landscape gardener here at Sterling's Fortune."
Robin.

"Good morning, mademoiselle," he said, hoping he
wouldn't find any kind of ring on her left hand. He
didn't, which pleased him. Still, a woman who looked
like Robin Harbin wasn't likely to be unattached. "It's
a pleasure to meet you…*again*."

"You've met before?" Kate's voice was filled with
interest.

"Briefly," Robin replied, her gaze still locked with
his. "Yesterday, in the rotunda. I was telling Mr. Beaudin how you like people to be on time for appointments."

Kate laughed softly. "Such a reputation I have."

"Sometimes," Robin said and smiled, "reputation is
enough to make an accurate assessment."

Amersen held her gaze. It was a very pointed remark, and they both knew it. She knew enough about
him to come to some kind of judgment. Certainly, it was
easy enough to click a few buttons on a computer and
discover who he was, since he spent much of his time
working social media to his advantage. But he knew
what she'd find if she dug a little. Gossip and innuendo.
Inflated facts about his lifestyle. Sure, he lived his life
to the fullest, but if he slept around as much as the
media reported, he'd have little time for anything else.

"And sometimes you shouldn't believe everything
you read," he said and smiled lightly.

"True. But I generally trust my instincts."

Amersen bit back a grin.

"So, Robin," Kate said quietly, "Amersen was just saying how he wasn't sure his image is enough to sell a high-end fragrance. What do you think?"

She looked him over again, and Amersen felt himself twitch all over. He was sure this woman, with her sexy drawl, worn jeans and gardening gloves, wouldn't have any kind of clue what it took to successfully market a product like an expensive fragrance.

But she didn't look the least bit overwhelmed by the question. She shrugged one shoulder and tilted her head a fraction. "Well, he's certainly attractive enough. *And* has a distinctive online status. All things considered, I can't see why it wouldn't be a successful venture. And sometimes good business is about risk, correct?"

Now Amersen laughed. "You know this, do you?"

Her chin came up, defiant and annoyed. "I know opportunity when I see it."

For a moment, he wondered if she was talking about the fragrance…or something else. The awareness between them was undeniable, and Amersen was astute enough to recognize a woman's interest.

"Yes," he said, briefly motioning to her appearance, "I'm sure you see much opportunity from your position out in the garden bed."

Her chin rose again, higher, more defiant, more annoyed. And then she laughed, as though she found him hilarious. "And I'm sure you're one of those men in love with the sound of their own voice."

Kate cleared her throat, as though sensing the sudden tension developing. "Ah, Amersen," the older woman said quietly, "Robin is more than simply a gardener. She has a degree in plant biology and often—"

"I'm sure Mr. Beaudin isn't interested in my qualifications," she said, gently cutting Kate off.

And she was right. He wasn't interested in her qualifications. But he was interested in *her*. More so with each passing second. "My apologies if I offended you, Miss Harbin."

Sure, he apologized. But he didn't mean it. And she knew it!

She waved an uninterested hand, but even that seemed fake and insincere. One thing about her—she couldn't take criticism. He bit back a grin, realizing they had a common trait, and decided he liked her more with each passing second.

"So...Kate," Amersen said and gestured to the folder in his hands, "shall we get back to business?"

The older woman nodded. "Of course." She looked toward Robin and smiled. "If you'll excuse us?"

"Certainly," she replied and glanced at him as though he was something unpleasant.

"Thank you for your help, mademoiselle," Amersen said and raised a brow. "It was most enlightening."

"Anytime," she said and smirked. "See you around the gazebo. Or not."

Then she turned and left the room.

"That's Robin," Kate said, as though to remind him.

But Amersen didn't need reminding. Earlier he'd made the decision to stay in Austin for a few days. He wanted time to think over Kate's business proposal.

And he wanted time to get Robin Harbin into his bed.

Gorgeous, yeah. Nice...definitely not! That was all Robin could think as she stomped her way back to the greenhouse, fuming from head to toe.

She was still steaming when Otis approached her half an hour later and said he would be spending the rest of the day in the small orchard at the rear of the big house. And still pissed an hour after that when she was elbow-deep in potting mixture in the orchid hothouse, slicing through the soil with a small, pronged fork. Using her pent-up energy made her feel better…and took her mind off a certain unbearable Frenchman. She'd made up her mind that she never wanted to see him again. Or speak to him. Or share air with him.

"Do you always attack your work with such…enthusiasm?"

Amersen.

Robin took a deep breath and straightened her back, then pivoted on her heels and turned to face him. He stood in the doorway, leaning on the jamb, hands in his pockets, jacket open and his tie a little askew. He looked like he belonged on a billboard and her treacherous, damned libido started jumping around like a jackhammer.

"Are you lost?"

He smiled a stunning, megawatt smile that did little to alleviate the way her blood was now surging through her veins from a combination of loathing and lust. She'd already decided she hated him and had no intention of changing her mind on that score. He could smile at her all he wanted.

"No," he replied flatly. "I was looking for you."

Her suspicions soared. "Why?"

"Because I think I offended you earlier."

She smiled übersweetly, plunged the fork into a pot and pulled off her gloves. "I'd have to care what you think to be offended, wouldn't I?"

"I meant no disrespect, mademoiselle."

"Sure you did," she shot back quickly. "You wanted to put me in my place, and you did exactly that. I mean, what would a mere gardener know about big business... right?" She smiled again, with so much saccharine sweetness it made her teeth hurt.

He laughed deeply, and the rich, sexy sound echoed in her ears. Damn. Why couldn't he be old and ugly? And not possess charm by the bucket load? And why had he come looking for her? It certainly wasn't for some half-meant, absurd apology.

"Let me take you to dinner to make up for my... offense."

He wanted to take her to dinner? Like, on a date?

She laughed out loud. "You're not serious."

"Perfectly."

She laughed again, this time without humor. "Ah, no, thanks."

"Do you need some time to consider the request?"

His formal, ridiculous manner turned her humorless smile into a scowl. "What I need, Mr. Beaudin, is to never see you again. Go away. I have work to do."

"Surely you must take a break," he said and pushed himself off the door frame. "If not tonight, perhaps tomorrow night?"

He strolled toward her, arms loosely at his sides, but with a stealth she found both exciting and annoying. She wanted him gone. "Give it a rest, *Amersen*," she said, using his name for the first time and stretching out the vowels with an exaggerated drawl. "Your blue eyes and sexy accent might work in the city, but out here in my greenhouse, there's no one to impress."

"Except for you."

His ego was astounding!

"I'm not interested in being impressed by you."

"Why?"

She stared at him. "Huh?"

"Why?" he said again. "Or rather, why not?"

"Because…" She was uncharacteristically lost for words. "Because I…"

"Are you married? Do you have a boyfriend? Lover?" He asked the question with so much self assured arrogance she couldn't help but gape at him. "Someone who might object to my…interest?"

Interest? She laughed out loud. "Really, can you hear yourself?"

"Perfectly," he replied, coming a little closer, so close that they were now barely a foot apart.

The air seemed to sizzle, and she fought the urge to step backward. She wasn't about to be outmaneuvered by this man. She wanted him to know exactly how she felt about him, maybe starting with a swift knee to the groin area. Which made her glance down, then up, and then realize she looked as though she was checking him out!

"I have… I have work to do," she said and fumbled over her words before meeting his gaze. "And I don't have the time to—"

"Have dinner with me," he said softly. "You won't regret it."

He was wrong. She would regret it. Just like she regretted the idea that she was actually considering it. Because, hell and damnation, he was absolutely the most gorgeous man she had ever met…and she wasn't the least bit immune to him. She was hot all over. Her entire body was about to be set on fire, as though he was the spark and she was the kindling.

She swallowed hard. "No. I can't."

"Robin," he said, her name almost sounding like

a caress. And thinking about his voice caressing her didn't help, either. Because all she could imagine was how it would feel if his hands did the same to her body! "Life is too brief to think about what we can't do."

She stepped back and pressed her hip against the table. "That's just your arrogance talking," she shot back. "Because you like to get your own way."

"Of course," he replied, not denying it. "I am a man, and we generally like to get exactly what we want." He shrugged, feigning innocence. "Perhaps you could make allowances for that."

She laughed again. If it weren't so ridiculous, it would be hilarious. "You're an egotistical snob…that's something I can't make allowances for."

He smiled, his blue eyes glittering. "I'll be on my best behavior, I promise."

"Go away."

He didn't move. "So, you didn't answer my question… about having a husband. Or boyfriend. Or lover."

The way he said the word *lover* made her skin prickle with a heady kind of awareness. Because he clearly had designs on the role. It was madness. They hardly knew each other. She didn't get swept away by good looks. Sure, Trey had been good-looking…but not like this. And she hadn't lusted after him the way she was silently and foolishly lusting after Amersen Beaudin.

"Not that it's any of your business, but I'm single… and happily so. However, I do have two older brothers and a father who would need only one word from me to come after you with a shotgun, Mr. Beaudin."

"You should probably call me Amersen," he said and then laughed so sexily her knees actually trembled. "Since we'll be going on a date."

"I'm not going on a date with you," she refuted. "Not ever."

"I can wait. I'll be in town for a week or so."

Robin planted her hands on her hips. "You can wait all you like…it won't make any difference."

"That's harsh. But you know, I think you'd like me if you gave me a shot."

She made a bored, huffing sound. "A shot? I wouldn't go out with you even if you were a prince. And not even if I had a fairy godmother who could turn a pumpkin into a carriage or even if I owned a pair of glass slippers."

He chuckled. "That's an interesting idea. You have a lot of spunk, Robin. I like that about you."

"I'm happy for you," she responded. "Now you can leave and go back to playing with your new perfume or writing one of your cynical and witty blog posts. Some of us have actual work to do. Goodbye." She said it to belittle and embarrass him. But he didn't look the least bit embarrassed or belittled. He looked amused. And cocky. He looked like insults weren't so much as a blip on his radar. He looked as though he could handle anything from anyone. Including her.

He reached into his pocket, pulled out his wallet and then tossed a small business card on the table. "My cell number. Call when you're ready to admit you want me."

Robin stared after him for several minutes after he left. Furious. Enraged. Appalled.

And totally—and unbelievably—turned on.

Chapter Three

"Robin, could you come up to the house when you get a chance? There's something I would like to show you."

"Of course," she said in response to Kate's request. "I'll be there in ten minutes."

It was early Wednesday afternoon, and Robin was glad for the interruption. She'd spent the last twenty-four hours deriding herself for allowing Amersen Beaudin to get into her head. Which made her even more determined to make sure he didn't get into her pants!

Foolishly, she carried his crumpled business card in her back pocket. Not that she intended on calling him. Not ever. But she didn't want to leave it lying around the greenhouse or her own home. The best place for it was the trash. And she'd do that when she got home. With that decided, she left her office and quickly headed up to the main house and walked through the back door.

Kate entered the room to greet her and suggested they go into the front lounge room.

Robin lingered in the large foyer for a moment. "The tree arrives tomorrow," she told Kate and waved a hand toward the staircase. "So I can start the Christmas decorations for you tomorrow."

"Okay, lovely," Kate replied.

"I know I'm running a little behind schedule," she

said. "The cypress I ordered wasn't available in the right size, so I had to find another farm to get the——"

"Robin," the older woman said firmly, cutting her off, "I know you'll have the house looking wonderful, just as you did for Thanksgiving, and for last year's Christmas celebrations. Sterling and I have the utmost faith in you, and you never let us down. Now, come into the lounge."

Robin stalled. "Is everything all right?"

"Perhaps you can tell me the answer to that."

Concerned, Robin followed her employer through the doorway and then stopped dead in her tracks. She hoped everything was okay. Kate looked serious, and that alarmed her.

"Ms. Fortune, I'm not sure what——"

"Perhaps you can explain this," Kate said and waved her hand in an arc, motioning toward the long buffet beside the fireplace.

Where she saw a pumpkin.

The biggest and brightest orange pumpkin she had ever seen in her life.

"It arrived half an hour ago," Kate said and pointed to a box beside it that was wrapped in white paper and had a silver bow attached to it. "Along with this. And there's a card with your name on it."

Robin approached the buffet and stared at the pumpkin and the box. She knew immediately, of course, that Amerson was responsible. The relevance of the pumpkin wasn't lost on her. She fingered the bow on top of the box and then slowly lifted the lid, gasping when she pushed aside a couple of layers of tissue paper and saw what lay within.

"Oh my goodness," Kate said, peering over her shoulder. "Are those what I think they are?"

Robin nodded and pulled her hand away. "Yes, I think they're exactly what they look like."

Glass slippers.

They were exquisite. She picked one up and held it up to the light, mesmerized by the way it shimmered. It was ridiculous. And at the same time, utterly romantic. Perhaps the most romantic gesture of her life.

"Are you planning on wearing them?"

It was *so* ridiculous that Robin couldn't stop laugher from bubbling low in her throat. "He's out of his mind."

"He?" Kate echoed. "So you know who sent them?"

She nodded and grabbed the card, pulling out a small square of cardboard and reading his dark, sexy scrawl.

I'm not a prince… I'm just a man who knows what he wants. Have dinner with me?

"Robin?"

Kate's voice jerked her back from fairy-tale land and forced her to regather her wits. "I'm sorry about this."

"Would you like to tell me what's going on?" Kate asked.

Robin sighed. "It's Mr. Beaudin's idea of a joke, that's all."

The older woman's frown disappeared, and then she chuckled. "Amersen, I see. Looks as though you made quite the impression."

"He thinks he's too charming to resist."

"And is he?" Kate inquired, brows angled.

"In his dreams, maybe. I'm really sorry about this," she said, embarrassed and increasingly uncomfortable. She didn't want her personal life intruding on her work. And she didn't want Kate Fortune to think that she was in any way involved with Amersen Beaudin. "I'll make sure nothing like this happens again."

Kate waved a hand. "There's no harm done, Robin. Just…be careful, okay. By all accounts, Amersen has something of a wild reputation when it comes to women. I'd hate to see you get hurt."

Robin managed a brittle laugh. "Don't worry about that. I have absolutely no intention of getting involved with him."

"Good," Kate said and smiled. "Sometimes it's easy to get swept up in romantic gestures." She pointed to the slippers. "Although they are quite spectacular."

Robin nodded in a vague way. "I'll ask Otis to help me get rid of the pumpkin," she said, feeling ludicrous having to say such a thing as she snatched up the box and card.

"It might make a nice Christmas decoration," Kate said and grinned. "Or a pie."

Robin chuckled. "Good idea."

"And what girl hasn't wanted a pair of glass slippers at least once in her life."

She couldn't help laughing brittlely as she left the room and then got back to work. Later, once she had the pumpkin and the slippers stowed inside her pickup, it was close to one thirty. She always finished early on Wednesdays and was glad to be heading home by two o'clock. Once she was inside, she dumped the pumpkin on the kitchen table alongside the shoe box.

And she seethed. She paced and cursed and muttered words she knew were usually heard in bar brawls. And she played with the business card twisting between her fingertips. He'd embarrassed her in front of her employer. And worse, he had made it impossible for her to *not* think about him every single minute of the day.

Damn him…

It was payback time. If he wanted dinner, she'd give him dinner. She'd give him a dinner he wouldn't forget in a hurry. The kind of dinner that would make a womanizing, commitmentphobic man like Amersen Beaudin run a mile. Robin grabbed her cell and quickly dialed the number before she had a chance to talk herself out of her craziness.

"Hello."

God, his voice was like being stroked along the spine with a feather.

"Okay…dinner," she said quietly. "But on my terms."

"Robin." He said her name on a breath. "It's good to hear from you."

"My place," she said and swiftly rattled off the address, specifics and directions. "Four o'clock."

Then she hung up before he could reply. And before she lost her nerve.

Amersen was intrigued by Robin's rushed request. And as he drove the BMW through a set of wide white-washed gates and down the long gravel driveway later that afternoon, he couldn't remember the last time he'd been so keen to spend time with a woman.

Of course, logically, he knew he was being foolish. He'd come to Austin for business. Not pleasure. But hell would freeze before he'd miss out on a chance to see Robin Harbin again. Particularly on her turf.

Still, he figured he was savvy enough to be able to mix business and a little pleasure without one overtaking the other. He had another meeting scheduled with Kate the following day and then a tour of the Fortune Cosmetics headquarters booked for the afternoon. He'd agreed to the tour only because he'd discovered that Graham Fortune Robinson was out of the city for a few days. He had no intention of meeting any of his half siblings while he was still considering Kate's offer. There was time for that later. Much later. Maybe never. The more time he spent in Austin, the less inclined he was to dig any deeper into his *family* background. And since Gerald Robinson had never made any attempt to contact him, Amersen figured he was better off not getting involved any more than he already was.

Which meant he had more time to concentrate on Kate's business proposal.

And Robin.

He eased the car to a halt, recalling the directions Robin had confirmed via text message. She lived in the small cottage behind the larger house, which was owned by her parents. The ranch house was nowhere near as large and imposing as the Fortune estate, but the place was tidy and looked well cared for. Amersen got out of the rental car and locked the door. He heard a dog bark and looked around, spotting a lazy-looking yellow hound peering at him from the side of the barn. There were chickens pecking the ground and a few head of cattle grazing in the paddocks to the right of the main house. He walked up to the cottage and noticed a note pinned to the door.

A. Meet me in the barn. R.

He grinned. It was cute. She was playing with him, and he liked it. The dog watched him as he walked toward the barn and then headed through the doors. There were horse stalls on either side, and Amersen saw her the moment he entered. She stood at the end of a row of stalls, pushing hay into a net. Wearing jeans, a pale chambray shirt, a sheepskin jacket and her purple cowboy boots, she was undeniably sexy.

"Have you ditched the limo?" she asked without turning, and he figured she must have watched him drive up to the house.

Amersen moved beside her. "I generally like to drive myself around."

She looked sideways. "Texas is a big place. Don't get lost."

He grinned. "I'm sure I could rely on you to come and find me if I lost my way."

She made a scoffing sound. "I think I'd just let you keep driving."

"You know," he said softly, trying to ignore the way his palms itched with a sudden need to touch her, "I don't really think that you would."

"That's because you don't know me in the least, Mr. Beaudin," she shot back hotly.

"I'd like to change that," he said, feeling the heat off her body almost as though she were pressed against him. "And I thought we'd agreed you would call me Amersen."

She met his gaze levelly, and her mouth twitched. "Did we?"

"Yes."

"Okay… Amersen… I'm going for a ride. Care to join me?"

"Horseback riding?" He looked around and saw there were two horses saddled and bridled and waiting in separate stalls. "You mean…now?"

"Sure," she said and grinned slightly. "Unless you're afraid of horses…or can't ride." She shrugged her lovely shoulders. "But I guess I thought a man as talented and successful as you could do just about anything. Of course, you must correct me if I'm wrong. If there *are* things you can't do, please, let me know."

There was pure, unadulterated challenge in her words. He glanced down at his pale gray business shirt, pressed trousers, suit jacket, hand-stitched Italian leather shoes and the wool Burberry coat he suspected cost more than she made in a month and then looked back into her eyes. She wanted him to refuse, to back down. She had something to prove, and making him look like a whiny, first-rate fool was clearly on the top of her list.

"Sure," he said and smiled. "Why not."

Her blue eyes sparkled. "Really? You can ride?"

He nodded. "A little. Let's go."

For a brief moment, he wondered if he'd called her bluff. But the challenge in her expression returned quickly, and within minutes both horses were out of their stalls and tethered to a hitching rail outside the barn.

"This is Blackjack," she said and ran a hand down the neck of the tall chestnut gelding. "He's all yours. Give him his head and not too much heel, and you should be fine."

"Should be?"

"Even the quietest mount can be unpredictable."

Amersen nodded, acted dumb and took the reins from her. "Thank you."

She looked him up and down. "You know, you're not exactly dressed for this. I'll understand if you change your mind."

"I think we both know that a Stetson isn't going to make a difference to my technique."

There was something oddly inflammatory about his words, and they both knew it. Amersen stared at her, feeling the awareness between them as though it possessed a life force of its own. He couldn't quite fathom his reaction to her. He'd known countless beautiful women and had bedded more than he cared to admit to, but there was something about Robin that affected him on a deep, impossibly intimate level. And ego aside, he was certain they'd end up in bed together.

She passed him a safety helmet that was propped on the fence. "You should wear this."

He glanced at the Stetson on her head. "I think I'd prefer one of those."

"Not on my watch," she said and placed the helmet in his hand. "Don't want to hurt that pretty head of yours, Mr. Beaudin."

"Amersen," he corrected.

She ignored him and headed back toward the stables, returning a few moments later carrying a pair of worn cowboy boots.

"They are my brother's but should fit," she said as she passed them to him. "I'm the kind of girl who believes in protection."

Amersen's skin heated. She was so damned provocative it was doing crazy things to his usual good sense.

He didn't quite understand it. Women never shifted his focus. One day…maybe, someone would. A decade from now. Once he'd truly made his mark on the world. Once his name and brand were renowned around the globe. And he still had a long way to go on that score, he reminded himself. Sure, he dated supermodels and dined with rock stars and politicians and had so many followers on social media he was known simply by his first name, but that could change in an instant. He knew that fame was a slippery slope. What he really wanted was his wine brand to be revered and served in the best restaurants and hotels in the world. He also wanted Noir to be *the* go-to place in Paris. He wanted it all. Everything that was his to take. If opportunity arose to build his brand and business portfolio, Amersen would do whatever was needed to be done.

Without being derailed.

But he felt derailed around Robin.

Big-time.

She smiled and grabbed the reins of the gray mare standing quietly beside the gelding. "This is Butterfly," she said and then quickly sprang into the saddle. "And she has been known to kick, so don't get too close to her rear end."

He watched as she eased the mare sideways and moved along in line with the corral. Amersen admired the way she looked in the saddle—like she'd been born to ride. After a moment, he changed into the boots, pulled on the ridiculous helmet, grabbed the reins and eased himself up and into the wide Western saddle. It wasn't what he was used to, but once he'd adjusted the stirrups, he was on his way, directing the horse in a line behind her.

He stayed back for the first ten minutes, following Robin's lead as they wound their way around the ranch house and down a gravel road between a couple of fenced-off pastures. There were a few head of cattle in one and several horses in another. The horses all looked up as they passed, a couple pealing out a long whinny, while one stood on point and snorted, beating the ground with a front hoof in an assertion of authority.

Blackjack whinnied in reply, and Amersen noticed that Robin's head turned immediately.

"Everything okay?" she asked, easing up the pace a little.

"Fine," Amersen replied and caught up, moving alongside her. "Nice day for it."

She glanced toward the sky. "It's chilly, but still good weather. I guess you're used to the cold."

"Of course," he replied. "Although I'm not a fan of cold weather. But a Paris summer is like no other."

She laughed. "Spoken like a proud Frenchman. Not that I've met one before you."

"I am proud," he said, shifting in the uncomfortable saddle. "One of my many charms."

She laughed again. "You *are* charming," she admitted. "Too much so. I'm not sure it's good for me to spend too much time with you."

"And yet," he said and grinned, "you invited me to dinner."

"It's the least I could do," she said and glanced sideways. "Considering you bought me a pair of shoes."

"Did you try them on?"

She laughed. "Do I look like a glass-slipper kind of girl?"

"I'm sure you could be anything you wanted."

When her laughter rang out again, an odd feeling pitched deep in Amersen's chest. He couldn't remember when he'd last spent time with a woman and simply enjoyed frivolous and flirtatious banter. Usually—no, *always*—there seemed to be an agenda. He worked and played hard. He didn't have time to waste on *getting to know* someone. And yet, he wanted to get to know Robin. Sure, he also wanted to get her into bed. But he enjoyed her company. She didn't waste time on flattery. She didn't pander to his ego. She was spirited and beautiful and had gotten under his skin in a matter of days.

"I'm curious," she said and glanced his way. "Where did you find a pair of glass slippers in this town?"

"I didn't," he replied. "I had them flown in overnight from New York. A friend did me a favor."

"A friend?"

"An actress friend," he supplied. "And I mean *just* a friend."

"None of my business," she said and waved a hand. "Still, didn't she think it was an odd request?"

"Nothing's out of the ordinary for Ortega."

"Ortega?" she echoed after a moment's silence. "*The* Ortega?"

Amersen nodded. "Yes."

"The Ortega who is one of the most famous and glamorous actresses in the world?"

He smiled to himself. Ortega was probably as hometown as Robin, since she had been born and bred in Montana and had clawed her way to a career first in Hollywood and now on Broadway in New York. Foolishly, he wanted Robin to understand that they were only friends, since Ortega was close to two decades older than him and a close friend of his mother's.

"She and my mother have been friends for a number of years," he explained. "They met before I was born, while my mother was traveling through Montana."

"I didn't realize your mom was American."

"She's not," he replied, thinking he'd said too much already. He didn't want anyone knowing that Suzette had spent time in the United States, especially Texas, or that she had once been au pair to Gerald and Charlotte Robinson's children. That would encourage questions he wasn't prepared to answer. "She's French, but she traveled a little when she was a young woman, before she married my father. She and Ortega stayed in touch when she returned to Paris. They've been friends since."

She nodded briefly. "And Ortega just happened to

have a pair of glass slippers on hand? Or is she used to you asking for movie props to impress girls?"

He laughed. Put like that, it did sound ridiculous. "It was my first time," he admitted and grinned, shifting in the saddle. "But I like that you're impressed."

"That's not what I said." She rolled her eyes and exhaled. "You really do think a lot of yourself. Must be freakin' exhausting."

He laughed again. Damn, she was intoxicating. "Why don't you have a boyfriend?"

Her gaze sharpened. "That's none of your business."

"Touchy subject?" he asked, easing up on the reins a little.

"No," she snapped back. "I did. I don't have one now."

"Messy breakup?"

She shrugged. "Aren't breakups usually messy? Unless you're one of those people who never lets anyone get too close because you're a commitmentphobe."

It was a deliberate verbal punch. "You've been reading the gossip mags." He chuckled. "Don't believe everything you see in print."

"Ever had a long-term relationship?"

Bang. No beating around the bush. "No."

"My point exactly," she said and clicked her mare forward. "Afraid of commitment."

She rode off ahead, urging the horse into a slow canter, and Amersen held his mount back, mesmerized by the picture she evoked. Her body moved in unison with the horse, her hips floating back and forth in a steady rhythm that was unbelievably erotic to observe. She rode as though she had been born in the saddle, her movements fluid and easy, and Amersen's blood heated.

He'd never considered himself much of a voyeur, but watching Robin was like a narcotic—utterly addictive.

Transfixed, he took a few moments to pull his thoughts together and then followed, clicking the gelding forward. The animal was smooth and responsive and it didn't take long for him to move up behind her.

"I'm not," he said when he reached her, so turned on that he lost his balance for a second.

She reached out immediately and took hold of one rein, steadying the horse as he scrambled to regain his seat. Amersen cursed under his breath and quickly got himself under control.

"You're not what?" she asked, releasing the rein.

"Afraid of commitment," he replied.

"Yet you admit you've never had a serious relationship. And you're, what?" she queried. "Twenty-five? Seems a little odd, that's all."

"Afraid of commitment and odd," he said, his mouth twisting. "My list of flaws is growing by the second."

She laughed, and the lovely sound flittered on the breeze. "Oh, god, don't get me started on your flaws. I could rattle them off for hours."

Amersen eased the horse back a little, conscious that his completely unsuitable clothing made keeping a firm seat almost impossible. "I really have made a bad impression. Obviously, the slippers weren't enough to change your opinion."

She shrugged lightly and maneuvered the horse left, following a narrower track that led toward an outcrop of rocks. "I'm not a girl to be swayed by gifts, Amersen."

"Then what?" he queried, smiling. "What's the secret to gaining your…affection?"

She laughed again. "Affection?" she echoed. "Is that what you're after?"

"I'm pretty sure we both know what I'm after."

She didn't even make the effort to look shocked or affronted. Her manner both intrigued and aroused him. In the past, women had gone to unbelievable lengths to hang on to his interest. But Robin Harbin didn't seem to care one iota if he was interested or not. And it made him want her more than he'd imagined possible. Of course, a little voice warned him, her ploy could be exactly that—show contempt and keep him hanging off her every word like a puppy dog. But instinct told him she wasn't made that way. Despite her temper and their constant sparring, there was something earnestly refreshing about her. And the more time he spent with her, the deeper he was drawn toward her sultry laugh and straight-talking conversation.

"Sex?" she queried, one brow arched.

He shrugged. "Who's to say what the future holds?"

"True," she said. "But I should let you know, I don't sleep around casually. I never have and I'm not going to start now. You might think I'm a flirt and easy… but I'm not."

"I don't think that," he assured her. "In fact, I think you're probably the most difficult woman I've ever met. Captivating…but challenging."

"Idiot," she said and laughed loudly.

Amersen laughed in response and then repositioned himself in the saddle as one foot slipped from a stirrup. "So, this secret, what is it?"

"Secret?"

"To garner your approval."

"There's no secret. Just be yourself."

"An egotistical snob," he said and moved up beside her, so close their stirrups clanged. "Isn't that what you called me yesterday?"

"It was exactly what you deserved."

"When I assumed you knew nothing about business and insulted you?" he reminded her. "You're right…I was an ass."

She didn't respond; instead, she clicked her horse forward and then urged the mare down a steep embankment. Amersen held the gelding back for a moment, then watched as Robin turned her head, and he noticed her expression was as daring as he'd ever seen. And defiant. He also knew she was waiting for him to bail.

Not a chance…

He turned Blackjack's head and headed down the ridge, holding on to the saddle horn even though he didn't need to, aware that she was watching his every move. There was an outcrop of rocks and several trees about fifty feet from the bottom of the embankment, and without consulting her, Amersen headed for them. Once he reached the shade, he dismounted and tethered the gelding to a low-slung branch.

She wasn't far behind and quickly had the mare hitched beside Blackjack.

"This is a nice spot," Amersen said and ditched the helmet, running a hand briefly over his head and grimacing when he realized his hair was plastered to his scalp. He shook his head and tried to reassemble his hair into something normal.

"Don't stress," Robin said and grinned as she took off her Stetson and hooked it over the saddle. "You still look good enough to have your face on a billboard."

"You know, I'm not as hung up on my appearance as you seem to think."

Her brows shot up. "I'll bet you spend more time getting spruced up in the morning than I do. A ponytail and some sunscreen and I'm done. I'm what you'd call low maintenance," she quipped.

Amersen's mouth twisted. "You're about as high maintenance as it gets."

She grinned a little. "I don't think I've ever been called that before."

"Not by your ex-boyfriend?" he asked, curious and not hiding the fact.

"Nope," she replied and perched her behind on a nearby rock. "Can I ask you something?"

He nodded. "Of course."

"What are you really doing here?"

"Here?" he echoed and waved a hand. "You invited me."

"I meant in Austin," she said. "Are you really considering Kate's offer? Or are you hanging around for some other reason?"

Amersen's back stiffened. There was no way she could know anything about his secondary reason for coming to Texas. The only people who knew were his parents and a couple of the Fortunes. As far as he was aware, Robin wasn't associated with any of the Fortune family other than Kate. But perhaps he was wrong. She could certainly be acquainted with Ben Fortune Robinson or Keaton Fortune Whitfield. He'd done his own digging when Keaton had first contacted him, and it appeared that his identity had been kept a secret from the rest of the family. Even that nosy journalist Ariana Lamont, who was writing an exposé on the Fortune children, didn't seem to know who he was—only that he existed.

"Some other reason?" he queried. "Like what?"

"Like…for instance…me?"

Relief coursed through his veins, and he took a couple of steps toward her. "Maybe."

"Then you're wasting your time."

He moved closer. "Considering we're here alone in this secluded spot, it doesn't seem to be a complete waste."

She got to her feet and pushed her shoulders back, which only enhanced her lovely curves. "Is this where you make your move?"

He chuckled. "Maybe. But I'm here at your invitation, remember? So my move, as you put it, is no doubt exactly what you expected."

"Maybe." Her blue eyes darkened as she looked him over. "But be warned that if you do, you risk a swift knee in the general direction of your junk."

He laughed loudly. "You sure about that?"

"Positive. Try me."

He was sorely tempted. But he also figured she wouldn't hesitate in carrying out her threat. "You know, you're the one who insisted we ride here, alone. If you want me to kiss you, Robin, you only have to ask."

"I don't want you to kiss me," she protested weakly. "Or anything else."

Amersen stepped closer and touched her shoulder, gently curling her toward him. He waited for her reaction, but it didn't come. Instead, she looked at him, meeting his gaze with a mixture of fire and ice in her expression. She looked as though she wanted to slug him and jump him simultaneously. "You sure?"

She groaned disdainfully and pushed away from him. "God, you're predictable. And I brought you here to—"

"See me fall on my ass," he said and raised a brow. "Sorry to disappoint you."

"You still have to make it back to the ranch," she challenged and strode back toward her horse.

"True," he said as he followed and noticed that her cheeks were tinged with color. "Tell me something, Robin...why do you dislike me?"

She looked at him. "I don't...that's the problem. I just don't like the fact that I..."

"That you want me?" he said, finishing her words. "As I want you."

She was breathing heavy. And she looked mad. At him. And with herself. "It's getting late. We should get back."

Then she was up on her horse and riding away from him without another word.

Chapter Four

Robin had always been told she had a fearful temper. And she'd never found that more accurate than when she urged Butterfly into a steady gallop and headed home. She gave the mare her head and let her stretch out, feeling some of her tension seep away as the breeze whipped her cheeks. In all her life, nothing had eased her moods like riding Butterfly. Not chocolate. Not alcohol. Not…

Not a few hours between the sheets.

And just like that, Amersen Beaudin was back in her thoughts. Again. It seemed she couldn't get him out. She thought about the sexy Frenchman when she should have been doing a dozen other things. And it had to stop. She was so annoyed with herself. Furious that she couldn't simply forget he existed and send him on his merry way.

She was back by the stables when she spotted Blackjack in her wake. And Amersen. Not walking. Not trotting. But heading toward them in a long, loping canter. He looked calm and comfortable in the saddle and as though he'd been doing it all his life, just as she had.

Damn. The man could ride.

He stopped barely a few feet from her and Blackjack

pulled up square, head at a proud angle, clearly attuned to the rider on his back.

Robin glared at the man still astride the big gelding. "You said you could ride a little."

He shrugged and dismounted easily, handing her the reins as he straightened his clothing and buttoned up his jacket. "It's been a while."

Her brows shot up. "Liar."

He chuckled. "Seeing you're such a fan of online gossip, I'm surprised you didn't pick up on the fact that my father is Luc Beaudin…a three-time Olympian and show-jumping silver medalist. I was raised around horses and could ride before I could walk—much like yourself, I suspect."

Robin felt like an idiot. She'd been so determined to make him look foolish, and all she'd done was prove she was petty and mean-spirited. "I'm mad at you. You belittled me and my work in front of my employer yesterday."

"I know," he said. "And I apologized, if you recall."

"It was a crappy apology," she said.

"I know that, too," he admitted. "But I'm trying to make it up to you. If you'd give me a chance."

"Why should I?" she defied, caught between a barrage of emotions she didn't want to think about.

"Because we're attracted to one another, and I'd like to find out where it might lead."

She harrumphed. "I know exactly where you think it will lead…to a proverbial roll in the hay. And I think I've made it clear that I'm not interested in anything casual with anyone."

"In my experience, everything starts off as casual."

Robin glared at him. It wasn't the beginning she was concerned about. Or the middle. It was the end. Because

Amersen had a reputation for having one casual relationship after another, and she certainly didn't want to be another notch on his bedpost, no matter how much her libido was betraying her and telling her to go for it. It would be incredible, she was certain. Great sex and a good time. But she also knew it would be foolish.

She grasped the horses' reins and walked toward the stables, hitched them both to their adjoining stalls and began untacking Blackjack. Amersen was beside her the moment she released the gelding's cinch, and he pulled the saddle off the horse's back before she had a chance. He was so close she could smell a faint trace of his cologne. Or maybe it was pheromones simply gone haywire. Whatever—every part of her was attuned to every inch of him.

"My ride, my responsibility," he said quietly. "Horsemanship 101."

Robin stood aside and watched as he grabbed a brush from the bucket by the stall door and used it on the gelding. She did the same with Butterfly, and ten minutes later, both animals were rigged with their horse blankets and led back into their stalls. Robin quickly made up their feed, and once they were fed, she closed the stall doors and turned back to Amersen.

His gaze was intense and burned right through her. She was sucked deeply in, feeling herself sway toward him almost involuntarily. He had a kind of magnetic energy she was inexplicably drawn to and couldn't resist. And then she was lost. All out of resistance.

She stepped forward and touched him, placing a hand on his chest, feeling the electric connection from the soles of her feet to the roots of her hair. As much as she wanted to fight it...as much as her head told her she was crazy to be within two feet of him, Robin couldn't help herself.

His hand came up and he touched her hair, twirling the strands between his fingertips. "Ask."

"Ask?" she echoed on a whisper.

"For this," he replied softly, coming closer. "Ask me to kiss you, and I will."

There was so much arrogance and self-assurance in his words, she wanted to slug him. But she couldn't. The heat from his body ensnared her, making resistance impossible. He wouldn't, she realized, ever take anything she wasn't prepared to willingly give. He had integrity. He had values. In some part of her mind, she compared him to Trey and realized that her ex had been just a boy compared to Amersen. He was a man in every sense of the word. He was strong and successful and very much in charge of everything he touched. Including her. But Robin sensed he lived by a code...only taking what was given freely. He wouldn't coerce her. And as she pressed closer, Robin realized he didn't have to.

"Okay," she whispered, all out of fight. "Kiss me."

He stared into her upturned face, and she memorized every handsome angle—his strong jawline, dark blue eyes, perfectly sculpted mouth and five o'clock shadow. He was breathtaking. And in that moment, hers to kiss.

His thumb moved over her nape, drawing tiny circles as he continued to stare into her eyes. She wanted to close her lids but didn't dare break the visual connection. Never in her life had a man looked at her in such a way. There was unmistakable heat and an electric intensity and pure, basic desire.

He moved and pressed his body against hers, drawing her closer. And she melted. Her hands crawled up his chest and curled into his shoulders and she parted her lips, waiting, anticipating, longing for his kiss so much Robin wondered if she hadn't lost her mind. She didn't do this…she didn't let a little harmless flirting turn into something more. Not ever.

But as his lips touched hers, Robin realized this wasn't like anything she'd experienced before. Sure, she'd been kissed and touched and more. But never with such scorching-hot intent. His mouth moved over hers slowly, instantly drawing a response, making her want even more. And then his tongue was in her mouth and the kiss deepened and she was clinging to his shoulders, rolling her tongue around his with pure, unadulterated hunger. He anchored her head and went in deeper, his tongue so seductive against her own she experienced a hot surge of longing down low, making her moan and then press her hips toward him. He was hard and clearly as turned on as she was.

"Give me half an hour," he muttered against her mouth. "Half an hour and I'll have you screaming my name."

He wouldn't need half an hour, she was sure of it. As it was, she wanted to pull down his fly, wrap her legs around his hips and let him plunge deep inside her, taking her wherever he wanted. Over and over. Until they couldn't think. Couldn't breathe. Couldn't stand. Couldn't do anything but feel sweat and heat and pleasure.

Except this wasn't the place, she thought as some faraway sound, like a screen door flapping, dragged a tiny part of her brain back to reality. Her parents were in the house. It was still daylight. They could easily be seen acting like a couple of horny teenagers.

She pulled on what was left of her good sense and dragged her mouth from his, breathing hard, and she stepped back, wrenching herself free of his embrace. He released her instantly, not looking anywhere near as overwhelmed as she felt. He looked his usual infuriatingly cool self. And he was smiling, as though he knew exactly the effect he had on her.

"Robin," he said quietly. "Breathe."

Her chest shuddered. "You're such a jerk."

"I'm a lot of things. But I think we just proved that we're going to be good in bed together."

She tried to laugh at his arrogance and failed. Her thighs felt like Jell-O, her girl parts ached, her hands were shaking and her lips throbbed from the intensity of their kiss. She didn't want to laugh. She wanted to kiss him again. And more.

But it wasn't the time or place. And Robin wasn't about to jump into bed with a man she'd known for only a little over forty-eight hours. Crazy, spirited and sometimes a little unorthodox she might be, but *easy*? Not a chance.

She'd brought him to the ranch to prove a point. Okay, so her plan to make him look like a failure on a horse had seriously backfired, but she still had phase two of her plan to put into action. Dinner with her sweet-natured folks...filled with enough parental pressure to make him grab his keys and run and never look back.

"I should make good on the dinner I promised you."

He smiled and dusted his hands together. "Can I wash up first?"

She nodded. "Sure. Follow me."

They left the barn and headed for the main house. She led him through the mudroom, conscious of his presence close behind her, and as they entered the kitchen, they were assailed by the aroma of her mother's famous pot roast.

"Our dinner," she said and managed a smile. "We'll be eating with my folks tonight," she explained and waited for his refusal. "I hope that's okay."

"Sure," he said easily. "I look forward to meeting them."

Robin noticed a tiny pulse beating in his cheek and realized he wasn't as cool as he was making out. Good. A dose of her parents over dinner *would* have him running out the door and back to his hotel within half an hour. Seeing as she hadn't brought a man to the house since she'd broken up with Trey, she knew her parents would be pumping out questions to Amersen over their meal. And she couldn't wait to see him squirm.

"You'll love them," she assured him. "They're wonderful people."

And right on cue, her mother entered the room. Veronica Harbin was the kind of mother everyone wanted—kind, considerate and always on hand for her children. A little on the plump side, she always wore floral dresses, cowboy boots, and tucked her curly blond hair behind her ears. Her mother was her best friend, and Robin loved her dearly.

"Mom, hi," Robin said cheerfully. "This is Amersen. He's staying for dinner."

She watched as her mother came forward and grasped Amersen's hand. "Lovely to meet you."

"Likewise, madame," he replied. "It is a pleasure."

Robin saw her mother flush. Like mother, like daughter, she thought, swooning over a sexy accent. "We've been out riding, so I thought I'd loan Amersen some of Evan's clothes."

"Of course," her mother said and smiled. "You know where they are. Dinner will be on the table soon, so don't be too long," she said and winked.

Robin grabbed his hand, ignoring the way heat immediately flared in her belly, and dragged him from the kitchen. Once they were out of earshot, she dropped his hand as though it was a hot poker and spoke. "How do you feel about a shirt and jeans? Mom hasn't cleared out my brothers' rooms, even though they left years ago. And you're about Evan's size."

"Great," he said agreeably.

Too agreeably. She knew he didn't want to wear her brother's old clothes. But he was too stubborn to say so. They were a lot alike, she realized. It made her long to stop being so aware of him. But he was right—they were attracted to each other. And their kiss had proved it. Who knew why they pushed one another's sex buttons? She'd never really understood physical attraction. If she did, she might have had a reason for Trey's infidelity.

She heard the television blaring in the front lounge room and knew her father would be watching his favorite game show before dinner. She beckoned Amersen down the hallway and up the stairs, stopping at the first door. Her brother's bedroom was exactly as it had been when he was a teenager—sports trophies on shelves, old posters on the walls. Evan still used the room if he stayed at the ranch for a weekend, so she knew he had spare clothes in the closet. Robin rummaged through the clothing and pulled out a soft plaid shirt, a pair of jeans and a lightweight Sherpa jacket.

She turned around and looked at Amersen. His suit and coat looked crumpled and grubby but redeemable, and she figured that a visit to the dry cleaner's should fix it. She passed him the clothes and shrugged.

"You can change in here. Meet you downstairs."

She left the room and closed the door, refusing to

think about how he would be nearly naked with just a wall between them. She waited at the bottom of the stairs, and when he opened the bedroom door and stood at the top of the stairs, she simply stared at him.

Oh, dear god, he was too gorgeous for words.

She liked the look of a suit on him. He carried it off effortlessly. But in jeans and her brother's plaid cotton shirt, he was out-of-this-world hot.

"I really wish you were old and ugly," she said and scowled.

He laughed and came down the stairs, his coat, suit pants, shirt and jacket flung over one arm. "No, you don't."

"I do. And just so you know, what happened in the barn isn't going to happen again."

"Sure it is," he quipped when he reached her. "You can't fight the inevitable."

"I can," she assured him. "You'll be leaving town in a few days and we'll never see one another again."

"Never is a long time."

"Never is what I want, Mr. Beaudin."

"Amersen," he corrected, reaching out to touch her cheek with the back of his fingertips. "You promised."

"You have to stop doing that," she said quietly and stepped back.

"Doing what?"

"Making me..." Her words trailed off and she glanced toward the living room and grimaced at the loud television, wondering what Amersen thought of the whole scene, because he seemed annoyingly relaxed. "Making me like you."

"I can't help it, Robin," he said, so softly she instinctively leaned closer. "Every moment I spend with you, I miss Paris a little less."

His words were provocative, sexy, and made her realize one incomprehensible fact.

I'm going to fall in love with this guy. I just know it.

And it was one big pile of fertilizer that made her the biggest fool of all time.

Amersen wasn't sure why Robin had invited him to dinner with her family. Maybe to make him uncomfortable? The truth was, he didn't do parents. Not ever. He never dated anyone long enough to form any kind of attachment, and back home he wouldn't have entertained the idea of meeting the family of someone he'd known for only two days.

Or likely ever.

But strangely, he sincerely *wanted* to meet her family.

Her father, Cliff, was a solid man who'd clearly had a stroke—he walked with the aid of a cane—but was very affable and chatty. Her mother was genuine and talkative and clearly adored her husband and daughter. Robin had a happy family. Much like his own, he realized, with parents who were genuinely in love with each other.

And while they sat at the big scrubbed table in the modest kitchen, talking about the ranch and horses, eating a meal that was homey and filling, and touching briefly on his business with Kate Fortune, Amersen could think of only one thing…that he ached to kiss Robin again. The memory of her pressed against him—of her lips and hands and lovely curves—was something he just couldn't shake. And he wanted more.

"So, Amersen," Cliff said and gave a lopsided grin. "You're going to sell perfume with Mrs. K?"

He noticed Robin's brows come together and smiled. "Something like that."

"She's a fine woman," Cliff said and nodded. "With a good mind for business. She might not be running the show now, but she's still the reason the Fortune family are big news in Texas. Don't let her age put you off... she's as switched on as ever."

"I won't," he assured the other man. "And thank you for the advice."

Cliff puffed out his chest. "Anytime."

Amersen saw an opportunity to dig a little deeper. What could it hurt to know a little more? "So, do you know the Fortunes very well?"

Cliff nodded and managed a half shrug. "I know Graham and Wes. Before the stroke got me, I used to breed and train quarter horses. I've sold a few for Pete's Place over the years," he explained, instantly jogging Amersen's memory.

Pete's Place, a ranch that took in troubled kids, had the name Fortune stamped all over it. Graham Fortune Robinson had spent years running the ranch, which helped teenage boys in need of a fresh start, until he'd taken over as CEO of Fortune Cosmetics. But according to some reports, the guy was still a rancher at heart and his appointment to the role by Kate had been a surprise. Still, he appeared to be doing a good job. Most of Amersen's other half siblings worked at Robinson Tech, the family corporation.

A place he intended to steer clear of while he was in Texas.

"The Fortune family is an important one, I gather?"

Cliff nodded. "For sure. Muddled and mixed-up... particularly since that whole fiasco with Gerald Robinson was exposed."

Amersen's back stiffened at the mention of his biological father. "Fiasco?"

Robin's mother spoke next. "You know, the thing with Gerald Robinson," she said, her voice quickly dropping an octave. "And his secret former life as Jerome Fortune."

"I'm sure Amersen doesn't want to hear all the gory details," Robin said extra cheerfully and cast him an apologetic look, as though her parents had somehow embarrassed her. "It's really none of our business."

Cliff nodded. "Can't help feeling sorry for Charlotte, though. Couldn't be easy finding out your husband used to be someone else *and* that he's got a bunch of illegitimate kids scattered all over the place. The man was busy," Cliff said and grinned at Amersen. "If you know what I mean."

"Cliff," Veronica admonished her husband. "That's not dinner-table kind of talk."

The older man patted her hand and chuckled. "Looks like I'm in trouble with my lovely wife. Still, all I'm saying is that I've been married for over thirty years and it's never been hard to stay faithful…but Robinson obviously couldn't help himself, since he apparently was with every woman he met, from his next-door neighbor to the babysitter."

Amersen stilled. *The babysitter.* His mother. Suzette. Au pair to the Robinson children for over a year. His chest tightened, his breath suddenly shallow. He was the product of that union. It made him sick to his stomach thinking how Robinson had seduced his mother and then paid her off once she discovered she was pregnant, and a familiar dread crept up his limbs and threatened to constrict his chest.

Breathe. Breathe. Breathe.

He swallowed hard and sucked in some air, willing his lungs to do their job and keep him from racing to the rental car to grab his inhaler from the passenger seat. The last thing he wanted was to embarrass himself in front of Robin and her parents by having an asthma attack.

He met Robin's gaze, saw her expression narrow and managed a small nod. She smiled fractionally, her blue gaze holding his, and oddly, it calmed him. He kept his stare steady with hers, pulling on all of his self-control to keep his breathing calm. After a few seconds, Amersen felt normal again, and he relaxed, the air filling his lungs steadily.

"So, how long you stayin' in town, son?" Cliff asked cheerfully.

Amersen shifted his gaze. "A few days," he replied. "Maybe a week."

The older man winked toward his daughter. "You should get Robin to show you the sights while you're in Austin. It's quite the town. We have some great restaurants and galleries you might like to see."

"Dad," Robin said quickly, "I'm sure Amersen has more important things to do, since he's here on business."

"Nonsense," Cliff said and harrumphed. "I'm sure you can take some time off to appreciate everything Austin has to offer."

Amersen glanced toward Robin. Yes, he certainly could. Since *she* was what he wanted. But he wasn't about to make any kind of inappropriate comment in front of her parents.

"You're right," he said agreeably and smiled. "If Robin agrees to play tour guide."

"And you should take a look around Sterling's Fortune," Cliff suggested. "It's quite a spread. Best ranch in the county. Maybe I'm biased, though, since my talented daughter is responsible for making the place look

so damned impressive. It wins awards, you know…
big-time stuff. Last year those fancy magazine people
came out and did a two-page story on the gardens and
how Robin was—"

"Dad," Robin said and groaned. "I'm sure Amersen
isn't interested in—"

"On the contrary," Amersen said quietly, cutting her
off. "I am very interested."

It was the truth. He *was* interested. In her. And somehow, it had become about more than simply sex. Sure,
he wanted to take Robin back to his hotel room, get her
into bed and make love to her all night long. He wanted
to touch every part of her and feel her legs tangled with
his. But he also wanted to hear her laugh. He wanted
to inhale the scent of her perfume. He wanted to order
room service and eat breakfast with her. He wanted…

To wake up next to her.

He wanted it so much he could barely think of anything else. Including the real reason he'd come to Austin in the first place. His business focus seemed to have
spectacularly disappeared.

He took a long breath and met her gaze. "You
shouldn't feel embarrassed because your father is proud
of you."

"I'm not," she said and smiled. "But you know how
parents can be."

He did. And he liked that she was talking to him as
though they were the only two people in the room and
that her parents were chuckling together. There was
something relaxed and completely normal about his
budding relationship with Robin. Stupid, he suspected,
to think of what they had as any kind of *relationship*…
but the connection between them was hard to ignore.

Cliff laughed and Amersen quickly got his derailed

thoughts back on track. "So, you were saying something about Gerald Robinson's secret life? I think I read something about it a while back."

The older man nodded. "Yeah…it's been big news in this town for a while. Looks like he turned his back on his old life as Jerome Fortune. I'm not sure anyone really knows why but him. But the secret kind of set down the pattern for a dishonest life, I reckon. He married Charlotte and had a family and managed to have several kids with other women. Like that Englishman who married that waitress from Lola May's… Francesca something… Keaton Whitfield is his name. I think he's added the Fortune name onto it now." Cliff frowned. "And then there was that Elliott girl…" His voice trailed off. "Can't remember her first name, though."

"Chloe," Veronica supplied. "She's a lovely young woman. She works as a counselor at Pete's Place. She got married recently, remember?" she prompted. "To that tall cowboy. You know him, don't you, Robin?"

Robin rolled her eyes a fraction. "Chance Howell."

Veronica clicked her fingers. "That's him. I think he works at Pete's Place, too. It seems like Gerald Robinson's illegitimate kids are coming out of the woodwork. It's like I always say, no good can ever come of lies and deception."

Amersen felt the stain of his conception creep over his skin. He nodded vaguely and shrugged. "Yes, I imagine you are right."

Veronica looked toward Amersen. "So, tell us a little about your family."

He glanced at Robin, saw her smile and then replied quietly. "Mother, father and a younger sister named Claire."

Veronica nodded again. "I suppose your business

with Kate will mean you'll be spending more time in Austin over the coming months."

As far as interrogations went, it was pretty mild. Still, he suspected that if he spent too much time in the Harbins' company, they would soon be asking him about his intentions toward their daughter. Upon reflection, he suspected his own parents would do exactly the same thing in regard to his sister, had she unexpectedly brought a man they didn't know home for dinner.

"Possibly," he replied.

They finished their meal, and Robin offered to do the dishes. Within seconds her parents were out of the room, having taken up Cliff's suggestion to watch television. Amersen collected a few plates and walked toward the counter.

"Damn," she said, grabbing the plates.

"Damn?"

"They like you," she said.

"Glad to hear it," he quipped. "But I'm not sure how you can know that."

"I know my folks," she replied. "They mostly let me live my own life, but they still like to give their stamp of approval on my...friends."

His brows came up. "We're friends now?"

"I'm not sure what we are," she admitted.

He stopped what he was doing and came around the counter. "Really?"

She stilled and turned, propping her hip against the counter. "Really. And I apologize if my dad's suggestion about me showing you the sights of Austin made you uncomfortable."

He laughed. "Wasn't that the purpose of the invitation...to see me squirm around your parents?"

She shrugged, not denying it. "Epic fail, though." She sighed lightly. "Doesn't anything faze you?"

"Not so far," he said and reached out, cupping her cheek.

"You know, I don't think I've met a more arrogant, cocky and self-assured man in my life."

"Thank you," he said, unashamedly turned on by her words. "Would you like to come back to my hotel tonight?"

She shook her head. "No."

"Can you deny that you want to?"

"What I want," she said and stepped back, "and what I'll do are two very different things. Look, I know women have probably been falling for your good looks and charm since you hit puberty, and I'm not going to deny that I'm tempted. But I'm also a realist. Once you leave Austin, I'll probably never see you again, and you'll probably forget that we ever met. And frankly, I don't want to be someone that gets forgotten so easily. I've had that recently, and it sucks. So, good night, Amersen. And thank you for an…interesting couple of days."

She stepped farther back, and he dropped his hand. He admired her honesty, even if he didn't want to hear her words.

"Good night, *ma chérie*," he said, feeling the space between them grow wider as she took another step backward. "Please say good-night to your parents for me and thank them for their hospitality." He gestured to the clothes he wore. "I'll see that these are returned."

"Goodbye, Amersen," she said, her choice of words clearly defining the parameters of their relationship. But he didn't say goodbye. He didn't say anything more. He simply pulled the car keys from his hip pocket, strode through the back door and left.

By the time he was in his rental car and driving away from the ranch, Amersen figured it was for the best. He was in Texas for one thing—to consider Kate Fortune's business proposal. Not to get involved with Robin Harbin. No matter how much he wanted to.

Business had to come first. It always did. He'd make a decision about Kate's offer and then head home to Paris, where he belonged. He had a couple more days, and then he'd be gone. No more Texas, no more Fortunes and no more bewitching honey blonde.

Still, that didn't explain why he felt so damned lonely as he drove back toward Austin.

Chapter Five

"All I'm saying is, don't be fooled by this guy."

Robin let out a long, impatient sigh and stared at her brother. She loved Evan, she really did, but sometimes he could be an overbearing pain in the rear end. And the last thing she wanted on Thursday afternoon was a pep talk from her older sibling, who'd made it his business to travel out to Sterling's Fortune to give her a lecture on whom she shouldn't or should date.

Pity he hadn't dished out the advice when she'd made the mistake of falling for Trey.

But this conversation wasn't about Trey. It was about Amersen Beaudin. Whom her mother had apparently mentioned to Evan on the phone earlier that morning. Then Veronica had raced around to Robin's house before she left for work and informed her that Evan had told her Amersen was some kind of womanizing playboy who bedded a different woman every week. He was a wolf. A shark. He was no good for her. He was going to break her heart. He was exactly the kind of man a good girl should avoid. Robin had listened while her mother offered a whole bunch of platitudes about the *wrong kind of guy*, and then Robin spent ten minutes telling her mother she wouldn't be seeing Amersen again, so there was nothing to worry about. Then she left for work, thinking the conversation over and done with.

Except the idea that she'd brought Amersen to the family ranch, where they'd all been born and raised, seemed to send her brothers into some kind of macho tailspin and resulted in Evan getting the short straw and visiting her at work to give her the aforementioned lecture.

"You're being ridiculous," she said and grabbed her tool kit from the table in the greenhouse. "I'm not being fooled by anyone, and for the last time, I'm not *dating* Amersen Beaudin. We went for *one* horseback ride, we had dinner with Mom and Dad, then he went back to his hotel. End of story. So, let up, will you?"

She wasn't about to mention that they'd made out in the barn. It wasn't anyone's business what she did, or with whom. Sure, the guy could kiss. But since she wouldn't be kissing him again, it made no difference.

Evan frowned. "Mom thinks you like him."

Robin rolled her eyes. "Really, what is this, high school? Go back to your office, Evan. I've got things to do."

She strode from the greenhouse, shoulders back, temper at boiling point and thinking that sometimes being the youngest sibling was unbearable. It took about two seconds to realize that her brother was following in her wake, still jabbering about how he'd done some research that morning and how Amersen was infamous throughout Europe and had a list of sexual conquests a mile long. She didn't want to hear it—for three reasons. First, it didn't make one iota of difference, since she doubted she'd see him again. Second, she wasn't going to take a lecture from her brother about her dating life.

And third, she didn't like how the idea that Amersen jumped from bed to bed made her feel.

"I'm just trying to help you see sense," Evan implored, following her into the house through the rear entrance.

"You're just trying to control my life," she snapped and kept walking.

She knew the housekeeper was upstairs, Kate was in her study working and Sterling was in town on an errand. Kate's husband had sworn Robin to secrecy earlier that morning when he told her he was planning on gifting Kate with a French bulldog puppy for Christmas and was visiting a breeder to make his selection from the litter. Robin knew Kate would be surprised and delighted by the gift, since she'd lost her previous and beloved pet some months earlier. She also knew Kate and Sterling wouldn't mind Evan being in the house, since they were acquainted with both her brothers and her parents.

"I'm trying to protect you," Evan said. "There's a difference."

Robin stomped through the kitchen and reached the main foyer area. The huge cypress tree had been delivered that morning and stood center stage in the middle of the foyer, extending several feet above the polished walnut balustrade on the second floor. Plus, several large boxes of garlands and decorations had been brought out of storage and were waiting to go up around the house. Christmas was barely weeks away, and she had mountains of work to do to get the house ready for the festive celebrations and the Fortunes' annual Christmas Eve party.

"Evan, you're my brother and I love you, but please stay out of my life. And leave, right now."

"Not until you promise you won't see him again."

She rolled her eyes irritably. "This isn't the eighteenth century, you know. I don't need your permission or approval to go on a date with someone. Or anything else."

His gaze narrowed. "So, you admit that you are dating him?" His frown deepened. "And what do you mean, *anything else*? Please don't tell me you're sleeping with some guy you just met."

Robin glared at her hypocritical sibling. Evan was handsome and successful and drew women to him like bears to a honey pot. Unlike the equally handsome but more serious Reece, whose wife had left him several years earlier and who seemed in no hurry to get back on board the dating train. "Really? I'm getting a lecture from a man whose bedroom has a revolving door?"

He didn't even try to look embarrassed. "See, I know what I'm talking about. Guys are only after one thing. And once we get what we want, it's over."

"You know, you really should give your sister way more credit."

Robin gasped slightly at the deep voice and turned on her heels.

Amersen.

He stood at the foot of the stairway, resplendent in trousers, a gray Aran sweater and a dark leather jacket. Feet crossed at the ankles, his arms folded, with one shoulder propped against the staircase, he looked breathtakingly handsome. Her heart did a foolish loopy loop, and she battled the way her knees weakened.

Robin saw her brother's back go rigid. "You must be the Frenchman."

"I must," Amersen replied, unmoving. "And you must be one of Robin's overprotective brothers…correct?" He pushed himself off the staircase and took a few steps toward them. "For the record, she's very capable of looking after herself. She's also not..." His voice trailed off, as though he was searching for the right translation. "Easy or promiscuous. You might want to remember that next time you decide to question her principles."

"I wasn't," Evan replied. "I was merely—"

"Sure you were," Amersen said, cutting him off. "You implied that she had jumped into bed with me. If she had, it would be no one's business but ours. If not, that's no one else's business, either."

Robin stood in stunned silence. Evan looked unusually uncomfortable and tugged at his collar. No one ever stood up to her brothers. They were alpha males in the truest sense. But Amersen could easily stand toe to toe with them and not blink. She should have been outraged by the absurd machoism emanating from both men... but she wasn't. She was foolishly flattered that Amersen had come to her defense. Because he was right—she could take care of herself. The fact he knew that and still managed to rattle her overbearing brother's cage secretly thrilled her.

"You should go," Robin said to her brother and hugged him. "I'll talk to you soon."

Evan looked as though he wanted to stay and argue the point, but to his credit, he merely nodded, inclined his head briefly toward Amersen and then left, retracing their steps toward the kitchen. Once her brother was out of sight and she heard the back door close, Robin exhaled a long breath.

"You're here?"

He nodded. "I had a meeting with Kate. She had to take a call, so I gave her some privacy."

Robin managed a tight smile. "It's...good to see you."

"But unexpected?"

She shrugged. "I expected you would continue to negotiate business with Kate."

"You said goodbye to me last night," he reminded her.

"I was making a point."

He laughed softly, and the sound reached her way down low. "I know."

God, he was so damned hot. He made her belly do backflips. She had a serious case of lust for Amersen Beaudin, as she was sure he knew.

"I had a nice time yesterday," he said and came toward her, standing on the other side of the pile of boxes. "Your parents are good people."

Robin dropped her tool kit and stayed opposite him. "My mother doesn't like you now," she announced, smiling extra sweetly. "Evan told her all about you, and now she thinks you're a player who has a different woman in your bed every night."

He fiddled with the open cardboard lid on the top box. "And what do you think?" he asked, not looking at her.

"Does it matter?"

"Probably more than it should."

His admission startled her and made her silently confess the obvious. She liked him. He liked her. A basic attraction between two people. It was simple chemistry. Alchemy. Sex.

"I bet you say that to all the girls."

He met her gaze. "I'm twenty-five, single and straight, and yes, I've been with many women. That doesn't diminish how much I want you. Or how much I respect your decision to not get involved any more than we already are."

His words stroked her skin like a caress. The man certainly knew the right things to say. He was smooth and seductive, even when it was broad daylight and they were separated by a pile of cardboard boxes filled with Christmas decorations.

A deep-rooted and acute surge of awareness raced through her body, and she couldn't fight the smile curling her lips. She didn't want to hear about his other women. She didn't want to listen to her brother or mother telling her how wrong he was for her. In that moment, Robin simply wanted to be a crazy free spirit and enjoy his company.

"Feel like helping out?" she asked and grabbed one of the boxes. "I have to start decorating the house today."

He frowned. "I thought you were a landscaper?"

Robin grinned. "I'm multitasking. I promised Kate," she explained. "And it's not any trouble, since I love Christmas."

"Me, too."

Robin stilled, midstride. "Really?"

"Sure," he replied. "What's not to love? Gifts, good food, eggnog, Christmas carols."

She smiled. "You go caroling?"

His mouth curled. "Well, no...but I appreciate it from those who do. Like my sister, Claire. She's the singer in the family."

"I can't hold a note, either. I mean, if that's what you're saying. And it's great to know you're not good at everything."

His blue eyes sparkled. "Who says I'm not?" he teased. "I'll have you know I can—"

"Stop jabbering," she cut him off as she passed him a box. "And walk this way."

He followed her obediently to the back of the cypress tree, box in his hands. "Couldn't you find a bigger tree?"

Robin took the box and placed it at their feet. "Oh, you know what they say. Size matters."

He laughed. "Is that what they say?"

She shrugged and then smiled. "Apparently. Not that I've seen a lot of…" Her words trailed off for a moment. "Ah…trees…you know, for comparison."

"No?" He smiled devilishly. "Trees in short supply for a landscaper?"

Heat rose up her neck. "I'm very particular about my…trees…that's all I'm saying."

"Really?"

Robin shrugged and ignored her hot cheeks. "So… about before," she said quietly. "And what you said to Evan, you know, about me not being…easy. Thanks."

"It's merely the truth."

"I know," she said and sighed. "But Evan is my big brother and thinks he gets to tell me how to live my life. You probably do the same with your sister, right?"

"Right."

She chuckled. "I like how you always say the truth. It's nice to know there are men out there who don't lie."

His gaze narrowed fractionally. "Your ex?"

"Liar of the century," she replied.

"What did he do?"

"Cheated with two other women," she replied and managed a laugh so brittle there was no mistaking it was fake. "At the same time." She laughed again. "And I mean, at the *exact* same time."

"So, he's an ass?"

Robin chuckled at Amersen's matter-of-fact description and the way his lovely cultured accent said the words. "You could say that. His parents own the ranch next door to my folks, so I've known him all my life. We were friends for a long time, and then for a while we were more. He's a bronc rider and was out on the road competing. I made the mistake of turning up at his hotel unannounced, and he had two women in his room with him."

Amersen's handsome face was expressionless. "What did you do?"

"Left," she replied. "Cursed. Cried. Then realized he wasn't worth my tears."

"I'm glad," he said quietly. "Tears would be wasted on a man too stupid to realize what he had."

She shrugged. "Trey was young and immature. Actually, I consider our breakup a lucky escape, since I'm sure both sets of parents were getting ready to send out wedding invitations."

"How old is he?"

"Twenty-five."

"The same age as me," Amersen offered lightly. "Not too young to know what is right and wrong."

"True," she said. "But you're a grown-up…and Trey isn't. Anyhow, enough talk about him. I need to get this tree, and this house, decorated."

His mouth twisted. "What can I do to help?"

"Pass me the red and green garlands," she said and pointed to the box at their feet. "While I climb up there," she added, gesturing to the tall ladder behind the tree. "Oh, and catch me if I fall."

Robin glanced upward and then started climbing the ladder. She was a few rungs up when she looked down and met Amersen's gaze. There was intensity and awareness and something else. Something she couldn't quite define. Until he spoke.

"I'll catch you," he said quietly. "I promise."

* * *

After a couple of hours of negotiation, Amersen agreed to the terms of Kate's proposal, and once he'd had his own lawyer look over the document, he was certain they would have a deal. The Amersen Noir fragrance would be unveiled the following autumn, coinciding with an aggressive worldwide advertising campaign that would include television, magazine and billboard exposure. It was a good deal, exactly the kind of thing he always looked for. It would be good for his brand and his bank balance. *And* it would mean he'd have to commute back to Austin over the next few months. It would also mean risking a meeting with any one of his half siblings. He couldn't shake the feeling that Kate knew more about that situation than she was letting on. True, she hadn't mentioned anything about Gerald Robinson to him other than a couple of offhand remarks about the man being Graham Fortune Robinson's father. There was no innuendo, no suggestive comments, nothing that he could pinpoint as the reason for his rising suspicions.

Just his gut telling him to stay alert.

And he would.

Kate's motives behind this proposition appeared to be genuine…but the bald truth remained that she *was* a Fortune. And he wasn't about to lose his edge of anonymity. When he was ready to face his DNA and his blood relatives, he would. Not before. And not yet.

"So," Kate said once she closed the laptop and sat back on the sofa. "Are you planning on returning to Paris right away?"

Amersen's thoughts were already out of the room. Earlier Kate had found him standing at the foot of the huge tree, handing garlands to Robin and making a slightly inappropriate remark about the shape of her behind, to which she replied by throwing a wad of tinsel at his face. He wanted to get back to the task. It was fun. And he didn't do fun often enough. He did business and he entertained celebrities and he wrote his blog and he slept with more women than he liked to think about, but fun…that had been in short supply while he'd been working on his business.

But Robin Harbin made him think about having fun.

"I thought I'd stay a few more days," he replied. "Perhaps take in a few sights."

"Alone?"

Amersen met her gaze levelly. "Your point, Ms. Fortune?"

"Kate," she replied. "And my point is Robin. She's a nice girl. But a little…let's say…impetuous at times. I'd hate to see that part of her nature taken advantage of."

Amersen wasn't the kind of man to kiss and tell. Or to take advice from strangers who seemed to be coming out of the woodwork. Still, he respected the fact that the people who cared for Robin wanted to ensure she was protected…even if, as in Kate's case, it was from herself. But he didn't think Robin was some kind of fragile flower who needed protection, and certainly not from him. She was strong and feisty and could give it back in spades.

"Be assured that I have no intention of taking advantage of anyone."

"I'm pleased to hear it," Kate said and nodded. "So, no doubt you will let me know when your lawyers have looked over the contract?"

"Of course," he replied and got to his feet. "You have the email address. Get your lawyer to send it to mine and we'll see."

He shook Kate's hand, thanked her, said he'd be in touch soon and that he would let himself out. He left the room and headed back down the hallway, hoping to find Robin on the ladder again. But he was disappointed. The tree was partially decorated and several boxes lay beside it, and he spotted her tool kit on the floor. However, he wasn't about to start searching the house for her. Amersen tapped one of the boxes with his shoe and let out a long breath.

Get a grip, Beaudin...

"If you're searching in those boxes for mistletoe, you're out of luck."

He stilled, then turned. She was behind him, hands on hips, her crazy, beautiful hair just begging to be freed from its messy ponytail and her blue eyes sparkling.

Amersen grinned. "Pity."

"Kate insists on the authentic kind," she said and dropped her hands. "Kind of how she likes the people in her life. So, I hope you're not intending to make her regret the deal she's got on the table."

Amersen let out a self-deriding laugh. "I'm not sure what I've done to have everyone think so poorly of me."

"Everyone?"

"Kate asked me what my intentions were toward you," he replied.

One of her brows rose steeply. "And what did you say?"

"Oh, I think I mumbled something about not doing anything untoward."

She laughed. "Glad to hear it. And if you want an answer to your question..."

"My question?"

She shrugged one shoulder. "About everyone thinking poorly of you."

"Oh…that. Sure, give it a shot."

Her eyes glittered brilliantly. "You're young, successful and in the public eye. You don't seem to care what mainstream people think. And your reputation with women casts a long shadow…right across an ocean."

"This bad reputation," he mused. "Did it occur to you that it's a fabrication?"

"No smoke, no fire," she said and smiled. "Like, how many women have you dated in the past six months?"

Amersen quickly did the calculation in his head and shrugged vaguely. "I'm not sure…a few."

"A few?"

"Okay…five."

"So, that's like one point two women every month," she said and counted on her fingers. "And of these women, how many did you sleep with?"

Heat crawled up his neck, and suddenly he felt like he was flunking morality school. "I don't… Well…a few."

"A few?" she echoed.

"Okay," he said and expelled a heavy breath. "Five. I dated five women and had sex with five women. Happy?"

"Am I happy knowing you bed every woman you date?" She shrugged and turned back to the ladder. "Not particularly. Am I grateful that you didn't lie about it? Sure."

"It's just sex, Robin," he said and tugged at his collar. "It doesn't mean anything."

"Precisely."

Amersen met her gaze, and the heat rising up his neck returned. For the first time in his life, he was being called out about his behavior toward the women he dated…and he discovered he didn't like it. Something burned in his gut, a kind of uneasy resentment that didn't make sense. Other than his parents, he generally didn't care what people thought of him. Writing *The Real Paris* had made him a target for regular online attacks of both his character and his personal life, but he always tuned out the gossip and innuendo. However, Robin's remark cut deep. Her opinion mattered. And he was annoyed that it did. They barely knew each other, and he shouldn't care one way or another. But the idea that she thought badly of him struck a chord.

"I guess I've never allowed myself to think of it as anything more," he said quietly.

"I'm not judging you," she said and shrugged.

"No?" he queried.

"You can do whatever makes you happy."

Amersen stilled and for a crazy moment wondered if she could somehow read his thoughts. There was a kind of bewitching quality to her, a mix of beguiling innocence and vivacity. Something about her drew him like a magnet to pressed steel. Something he didn't understand or want. In a matter of days, he'd be gone. Getting involved any deeper was foolish. And he'd never considered himself a fool…until now.

"I was just thinking that," he admitted softly. "I was thinking that I didn't give much thought to being happy these days."

Her gaze narrowed. "Why not?"

He shrugged one shoulder. "Too busy. Too many meetings. Too much ambition. All of the above. But…" He paused, looking around, gesturing a hand in a vague arc. "Hanging out here, with you…that makes me happy."

As soon as he said the words, he felt like snatching them back. Her eyes were suddenly huge in her face, her cheeks blotched with color, and she took a step backward. "I...uh...I need to get back to work."

Amersen gave himself a mental shake. "Sure. Take care, Robin."

She turned around and spoke as she climbed the ladder. "Yeah...you, too."

"The tree looks good, by the way," he said.

"Thanks," she said and climbed higher, her voice raspy. "So long."

Amersen lingered for a moment, then realized she wasn't going to say anything else. He opened his mouth to speak and quickly changed his mind. He was cursing himself for being foolish as he left the house, and still giving himself a lecture about being attracted to a woman who clearly wasn't interested in anything other than a mild flirtation as he headed into town.

When he reached his hotel in the city, it was after three o'clock. He pulled up outside the hotel and handed the car keys to the bellhop. Amersen was striding across the foyer when the concierge approached him and handed him a message, handwritten in a scrawl he didn't recognize. As he read the words, his entire body stilled.

Heard you were in town. Would like to catch up.
Keaton Fortune Whitfield.

Damn.

There was a cell number at the bottom of the note. Figuring it wasn't too early for a drink, Amersen headed for the bar. He ordered a belt of scotch and sat alone in the corner. The place was deserted, and it gave him time to think.

So, his half sibling had somehow been tipped off to his arrival in Austin.

Amersen wasn't sure how. He'd kept his movements under wraps—hadn't posted any activity on any of his social media accounts. No one except his family, his lawyer and two of his closest friends in Paris knew of his whereabouts. And he trusted them implicitly. Other than having his assistant back in Paris use his real name to rent a car and book the hotel, he'd flown under the radar. Even his visit to the Fortune Cosmetics Headquarters had taken place in the evening and with some secrecy. Only Kate and a pair of security guards had been with him.

Then he remembered that Robin's brother had been sniffing around for information about him on the internet…maybe there was some connection? From what her parents had said when he'd been there for dinner, it was clear the Harbins knew Keaton and several of the other Robinsons. His head hurt thinking about it, and he'd just decided to order another drink to drown his woes when his cell pinged, indicating he had a text message. He'd bloody well be heading back to Paris on the first flight he could get if Keaton Fortune Whitfield had somehow managed to access his cell number.

But it wasn't his half sibling.

It was Robin.

Dinner. Friday night. Seven o'clock. My place. Parent-free zone.

He smiled. Paris could wait.

Chapter Six

Without anyone telling her so—notably because she hadn't breathed a word to anyone—Robin knew by late Friday afternoon that she was asking for all kinds of trouble by inviting Amersen to dinner.

And yet…she couldn't help herself.

Hanging out here, with you…that makes me happy.

His softly spoken words banged around in her head and she mentally sighed every time she thought of them. Damn, the man *so* knew how to get under her skin. Maybe it was deliberate? Perhaps that was how a smooth, charming player got women into his bed? Good sense would say so. So would online gossip. And yet he didn't seem that manipulative. He seemed genuine. In that moment, he'd seemed so achingly vulnerable— and it had done something almost indescribable to her raw defenses. She couldn't pinpoint the feeling, and her logic didn't want to. But within an hour of him leaving the ranch, she'd made a decision.

To hell with good sense.

She liked him. She enjoyed being with him. So what harm could a night in, some dinner and conversation really do? It didn't mean she was about to jump into bed with him. It didn't mean that she would lose her heart to the man. It was just dinner.

No big deal.

"Something special going on tonight?"

Robin looked up from her place behind the counter in her small kitchen. Her mother stood at the back door, apron tied around her waist, arms folded.

She shrugged lightly. "Just making spaghetti sauce."

"You're not joining us tonight?"

Since she'd broken up with Trey, Robin had eaten dinner with her parents most Friday nights, since most of her friends wanted to head into Austin to enjoy the nightclub scene and drink and party until dawn. Not that she was averse to dancing and a beer or two after a week of hard work, but she really was more stay at home than party hard, so Friday dinners with her parents usually suited her fine.

"Uh, no," she said and stirred the sauce simmering on the burner. "I've got company tonight."

"The Frenchman?"

Robin smiled to herself, thinking how quickly Amersen had fallen from grace in her mother's eyes, thanks to her interfering brother. "Yes, Amersen."

"Be careful, okay?"

She met her mother's concerned gaze. "I will, I promise. And he's still the same person you thought was a good sort of man a few days ago. I'm not in danger here, Mom, so you can stop worrying."

Her mother let out a brittle laugh. "I'll always worry. When you have children of your own, you'll know why."

Robin did want children, but her plan had always been to have them some years in the future. For a while she'd believed she'd have them with Trey, but that idea was now out the window. She never wanted to see him again, let alone anything else. And since the only other man on the horizon at the moment would be returning to Paris within days, Robin suspected it was time she seriously got back into the local dating scene.

"Kids are way off into the future, Mom. And you can rest easy knowing that Amersen will be leaving in a couple of days now that his deal with Kate is in writing."

Veronica Harbin didn't look quite convinced, but she nodded. "Okay. I'll see you tomorrow."

"Sure," Robin said.

Once her mother left, Robin turned the heat under the pot to low and headed for the bathroom. Half an hour later she was showered and dressed in jeans, a soft purple sweater and a pair of sparkly moccasins she'd bought from a craft market recently. She'd washed and dried her hair, leaving it to hang down her back and shoulders, played around with a little makeup and then walked from room to room in the house for half an hour waiting for him to arrive.

He turned up at three minutes to seven and stood on her doorstep, a bottle of wine in one hand and a small wrapped box in the other. And he looked so gorgeous he stole her breath. In dark trousers, a black shirt open at the throat and a leather jacket that hugged his broad shoulders, he looked totally handsome and masculine. And hot.

"Another gift?" she remarked as he crossed the threshold and she closed the door behind him.

He shrugged lightly. "It's just a small thing, *amoureuse*."

Robin wasn't exactly sure what that meant, since she didn't speak a lick of French, but she could guess it was some kind of endearment, which made her as giddy as a teenager in the midst of a first crush. And since he smelled absolutely divine, her giddy senses did a crazy loop-de-loop.

She met his gaze as he passed her the box. "Thank you. Let's go into the living room."

He followed her down the hallway and stalled in the doorway to the living area. And he was smiling as he looked around the room, eyes wide.

"Too much?" she asked.

The huge, fluffy spruce tree, complete with an assortment of gifts beneath it, took up most of one corner, and the rest of the room was decorated within an inch of its life. Garlands were looped along the picture rail, and bunches of fresh holly sat in several vases on the table behind the sofa. A ceramic nativity scene lay beside the fireplace, complete with straw, backlighting and a timber manger her father had made for her years ago. And there was an array of mismatched ornaments and festive novelties on the mantel, including the glass slippers he'd gifted her.

"No," he replied, still smiling. "Exactly what I imagined."

Robin's skin prickled with awareness. "I told you I like Christmas."

"So you said," he remarked and pointed to the small box in her hand. "Which is why I got you that."

Robin fiddled self-consciously with the ribbon on the top of the box for a second and then opened the gift. It was a snow globe depicting the Eiffel Tower in front of a skating pond, complete with tiny skaters, snow, reindeer and a sleigh. Paris at Christmastime. Her heart skipped a beat as she held it in her hand.

"It's…lovely," she said and turned it upside down, turning the small key on the base. Music began, a sweet, familiar melody. "I know this song… It's…it's…"

"Douce Nuit," he supplied. "'Silent Night.'"

"Of course," she said and smiled. "Thank you. Another favor from Ortega?"

He grinned. "Not this time. I was out looking around the city this afternoon and ended up in a place called South Congress. I found it in one of the stores there."

"SOCO is known for being a little on the quirky side," she explained and placed the globe on the mantel. "It has some great little restaurants and places for live music. In fact, there are several good nightclubs in Austin, if that's your thing."

"I suppose you could say nightclubs are my thing," he said. "Since I own one."

She nodded. "Yeah, I read about that online. Quite a popular place you've got there…home away from home for celebrities."

"I have a no-paparazzi rule between ten and midnight, so yes, some celebrities come to unwind and keep out of the way of journalists looking for a scoop. The European tabloids can be mercenary."

"That's why I would never want to be famous," she said and chuckled, thinking that Amersen was probably the most famous person she'd ever met. "I'm happy to live my low-key, middle-class, small-town life in my little house with its cottage garden. Which probably makes me sound as dull as a door."

"Nothing about you is dull."

Robin could barely stand the intensity of his gaze, and she swallowed hard. "I should probably check on dinner. We can open that wine if you like."

"Certainly," he said and followed her into the kitchen.

Robin put water on to boil for the pasta, grabbed a couple of glasses from the cupboard and placed them on the countertop, then pulled the corkscrew from a drawer, handing it to him. "Is that from your winery?" she asked.

His brows rose. "You've done some digging."

She half shrugged. "Type your name in a search engine and pages of stuff come up. I read a little bit here and there, including something about the winery and nightclub and how you've made a lot of money."

"The money is merely the by-product, not the motivation."

She chuckled. "I wasn't criticizing. Although making off-the-cuff remarks about the unimportance of money does seem to be a privilege of the rich."

He took off his jacket and draped it on the back of a chair and then uncorked the bottle and poured wine into the glasses. "Elitist."

Robin laughed. "You're the snob, not me. Tell me about your family."

He came around the counter and passed her a glass, which she held in one hand while she stirred marinara sauce. "I have a younger sister, Claire, who is studying business at university. My father, Luc, is a professional equestrian and my mother, Suzette, sells real estate."

"And you," she added. "Handsome and successful and soon to be the face of Fortune's next big thing."

"We'll see."

She frowned. "Are you having second thoughts?"

"No," he replied. "But nothing is ever a done deal until the deal is done. I never take opportunity for granted, although in this instance I am not entirely convinced that my image alone can sell a product in a market that is so fiercely competitive."

Robin sipped her wine. "Kate believes in you. And so do I," she added, then felt foolish. "Not that my opinion matters."

"On the contrary," he said and turned, resting his hip against the counter, so close she could feel the heat coming off him. "Since you are my only friend in Austin, your opinion does matter."

She stopped stirring the sauce and turned, facing him, barely inches apart. "I don't think I've ever been anyone's only friend before. That's a big responsibility." She plonked a wad of spaghetti into the now boiling water.

His eyes glittered. "Tell me something. Just before, you said you were happy here, with your life, living here. Do you not have any interest in seeing the world?"

Robin didn't let her gaze slide from him. "I would like to travel at some point. But although Kate is a generous employer, a landscaper's salary doesn't usually stretch itself to regular vacations abroad. But who knows," she mused. "One day I might get to check a few places off my list."

"Your list?"

"My Christmas list," she said and shrugged. "I've always had this crazy idea that I'd like to spend Christmas in different cities around the world. You know, like a wintry English Christmas in the Lake District…or a warm Christmas on a Sydney beach." She laughed at herself. "It sounds silly."

"Not at all. It sounds like…fun."

There was that word again. The one he'd used to describe being around her. "It's a shame you're leaving soon."

"Yes," he said quietly, and suddenly the mood between them became intensely intimate. "You could come back with me…stay for a while…tick Paris off that list of yours."

Robin's jaw dropped. "Huh?"

He shrugged his broad shoulders. "Paris is a city like no other, and at Christmas it really does come alive. There are more lights than usual on the Champs-Élysées and Saint-Germain. Street vendors at their carts sell roasted chestnuts, and the scent seems to stay in the air for weeks. And there are stalls and markets that pop up like mini villages, for the locals and the tourists alike, offering glacé fruit and cheeses and wine from every province in the country. You might find a brass band on a street corner, playing festive music. And on Christmas Eve, as the daylight fades, the Eiffel Tower comes alive with thousands of glittering lights that seem to cast a warm glow across the entire city."

Robin's bones liquefied. She could listen to Amersen's sexy voice for hour upon hour and never grow tired of the way his accent made every word sound like a seduction. And he made Paris sound so inviting she was almost tempted to accept his offer.

"It sounds…wonderful."

"It is my home. Where my heart is, *tu vois*?" His gaze burned into hers. "Do you see?"

"Like my heart is here." She felt the heat of the awareness between them, like flames licking at her.

"Then we are…*condamnés*," he said, taking the glass from her hand before he translated. "Doomed."

Robin had never felt more aware of a man in her entire life. And they'd barely touched. Barely kissed. But she was so drawn to him it was terrifying. And thrilling. She managed a soft laugh. "You might be doomed after you sample my cooking."

"No risk," he said and placed his glass on the counter. "No reward."

Then he curled a hand around her nape and gently

urged her closer, closing the space between them. And then he kissed her. Softly. Slowly. Sensually. Like he had all the time in the world. Like they weren't doomed. Robin closed her eyes and pressed closer and kissed him back, accepting his tongue into her mouth as though it was all she needed to exist. She couldn't remember ever being kissed with such gentle finesse and yet such gut-wrenching passion. That was the difference between him and any other man she'd kissed. Amersen Beaudin wasn't kissing her to seduce her into bed. He was kissing her because it felt damned good. His hands didn't roam, didn't grope, didn't do anything except steady her. And his warm, seductive mouth had a power she couldn't believe.

When he lifted his head and pulled back a little, she was breathing hard, her eyes now open, the blood in her veins on fire. "That is not so much against the rules, no?"

"No," she muttered, smiling at the way he mixed up the words. "Yes."

He smiled and stepped back. "Then you should probably feed me some of your bad cooking."

Robin took a steadying breath, forced some guts into her knees and quickly finished the meal preparations. The table was already set, the salad was in the refrigerator and the bread cut up and in a basket on the counter. Within minutes she had the spaghetti, salad, Parmesan and bread on the table and invited him to take a seat. He grabbed the wine and refilled their barely touched glasses before he sat down.

His eyes kept steady with hers. "Tell me about the purple."

So he'd noticed. "I always wear something purple,"

she said and shrugged. "I've been doing it since I was a kid. No real reason... I just love purple."

He ate some pasta and then rested his fork on the plate. "You weren't wearing purple the first time I met you...remember, in the gazebo. You had on that white dress."

"Purple thong."

He almost choked on his meal. "Oh...I see." He groaned softly. "Now I have that image fixed in my brain...*merci*."

"The dress?" she queried. "Or the thong?"

"Both," he replied. "You know, I haven't seen you in a dress since. Not a fan?"

She shrugged. "I'm always digging in the dirt—that's more of a jeans and T-shirt kind of job. I'm not much of a fashionista, anyway. And I don't go out much these days, so no real need for playing dress up. I'm on the short, curvy side of the spectrum, so not exactly made for fancy gowns. Not like those skinny European models you date, I guess."

"Actually, the last woman I dated was five foot three and works as a viticulturist," he said quietly. "That's someone who—"

"I know what they do," Robin cut him off irritably. "It's someone who decides what grape varieties to plant and handles pest management, irrigation and deciding the best time to harvest the grapes."

"Yes, exactly."

She speared some spaghetti. "So, you broke up. Why?"

He shrugged lightly. "We dated for a while. She wanted...more."

Robin looked up and met his gaze. "Oh...*commitment*. How frightening for you."

His cheeks darkened. "I wasn't ready for anything serious at the time. And I never lied to her about a future."

"Just long enough to get her into bed, I imagine."

"I never lied," he said again, his mouth suddenly a thin line. "Not all men stoop to lies and deception, Robin."

It was a deliberate hit, and she sat up straight in the chair. "I know that. I've had a good role model in my own father to know the difference. Like you have, I suppose."

"Luc Beaudin is my stepfather."

Robin stared at him, eyes wide. "Oh…I didn't know that."

"No one knows," he said quietly. "Except my parents and sister."

Robin swallowed hard, reeling in the weight of his admission to her. "And your real dad?"

His gaze narrowed. "Luc *is* my real father," he shot back quickly. "At least he is in every way that counts."

"Of course," she corrected quickly. "I just mean, your biological father."

"A sperm donor," he replied baldly. "Nothing more."

"Have you ever met him?"

Amersen had no real idea why he'd told Robin something he'd never even discussed with his closest friends. It was the most private part of himself, like a shadow he tried to dodge at every opportunity. Although he'd always known Luc wasn't his birth father, it wasn't until he was sixteen that he'd demanded to know who the other man was. That was when his mother had told him an abridged version of the truth—that he was conceived from a brief affair she'd had while in America and that his biological father was a wealthy married man who had another family and would never leave his wife. She'd never said who he was, and Amersen hadn't asked. What did it matter after so many years? It wasn't until he was contacted by Keaton Fortune Whitfield and Ben Fortune Robinson and found out he was *Gerald Robinson's* biological son that all his previously concealed resentment had surged to the surface.

Because he hated the fact he was Gerald Robinson's bastard child.

He hated it so much he could taste the hatred on his tongue and feel it burning through his veins. And he'd never admitted that fact to anyone, not even his mother, not even once he knew the whole truth about who he was, after she told him how she'd convinced Robinson she'd *taken care* of her pregnancy and the man had been relieved. Because twenty-five years ago Robinson hadn't been prepared to acknowledge Suzette's child as his own...and now Amersen wasn't prepared to acknowledge that other man as his father.

"No," he said, answering her question. "I've never met him."

"And you've never told anyone?"

He shrugged and feigned interest in the food on his plate. "Never."

Amersen expected her to ask him why he admitted such a thing. But she didn't. Instead, she reached across the table and placed a steady hand on his forearm. He could feel the warmth of her touch through his shirt, the connection somehow like a tonic that eased away any regret he had in telling her. And suddenly, the rest of the story teetered on the edge of his tongue, anxious to be told.

"You can trust me, Amersen. I won't betray your confidence."

He glanced up and met her gaze. She drew back her hand and continued eating her meal, but Amersen was achingly conscious of the undercurrent of awareness between them. It was impossible to ignore the fact that they were drawn to one another. And he wanted more of her. Despite knowing he was leaving in a matter of days.

"Would you spend the day with me tomorrow?"

She took a breath, and he was sure he heard a tiny shudder and prepared himself for her refusal. Of course she should. That would be the sensible thing to do.

"Yes," she said. "I will."

"I'll pick you up at eight and we can head into town for breakfast," he said and then gestured to the plate in front of him. "Incidentally, you're not a terrible cook. This is *très bien*…very good."

"Thank you," she said. "You're very sweet."

"Sweet?" Amersen laughed and drank some wine. "I don't think anyone has ever called me that before."

Robin's face lit up in a lovely smile. "For the record, that doesn't mean I'm going to sleep with you tonight."

Amersen cast her an earnest look. "I know this," he said and reached out to grasp her hand, lightly stroking her palm. "I have no illusions, Robin. I'll be returning to Paris soon, and the last thing I wish to do is hurt you in any way. But we can spend time together as friends, *oui*?"

"Oui," she said and smiled. "Yes." Her fingertips curled around his. "After all, I *am* your only friend in Austin."

He tugged her hand toward his mouth and gently kissed her knuckles. "True."

"So maybe you should stop doing that," she said and pulled her hand away. "Even though it's very…nice."

"Sweet? Nice?" Amersen made a face. "*Mon Dieu…*

I have clearly lost my…" His voice trailed off as he searched for the right word.

"Mojo?" she suggested and laughed, dipping a chunk of bread into the sauce on her plate. "Rest assured, Amersen, you are as charming as ever. And tempting. And if you weren't leaving in a matter of days, I would probably drag you into my bedroom right now and have my way with you. But you are. So I won't."

God, he loved her honesty. It was like a blast of fresh air every time she spoke. She kept talking, about Christmas and needing to go gift shopping, and as he listened to her lovely voice, he realized he'd never been more attracted to a woman in his life. And he tried not to think about how all the blood in his body had surged to the lower half of his anatomy when she'd mentioned them having sex. He wanted to make love to her so much he could barely concentrate on what she was saying.

While she made coffee and prepped dessert, Amersen remained in his seat, elbows on the table, his chin resting on his linked hands, listening contentedly to her almost musical voice and thinking he'd never met a woman with more beautiful hair. It was long and lustrous, cascading down her back in a wave. He wanted to run his fingers through it, to anchor her head and kiss her again and again and taste the sweetness of her lips against his own.

"Texas sheet cake," she said and placed a small plate in front of him, along with a steaming mug of coffee. "Kind of like a brownie, but gooier and delicious. Try it," she offered and licked a little chocolate frosting off her thumb. "Trust me, once you taste it, you won't go in for those fancy French desserts like crème brûlée or éclairs ever again."

Amersen wasn't about to tell her he didn't like desserts all that much. Her sheer enthusiasm meant he'd spoon sugar into his mouth rather than curb her animation. He tasted the cake, ignoring the way the sugary sweetness wreaked havoc on his palate, doused it with a sip of coffee and then smiled. "Yes…very good."

She smiled back, as though he'd gifted her some great compliment. "So, what will we be doing tomorrow?"

He shrugged lightly. "Breakfast. Shopping. Taking in the sights. I thought you could show me around this town of yours."

"Deal," she said and grinned. "And I'll take you to a gift shop so you can take some souvenirs home. Nothing screams Texas more than a baseball cap in the colors of the state flag. Although it might ruin that sexy, just-tumbled-out-of-bed hair of yours."

He grimaced. "Perhaps I'll stick with a key ring instead."

"Oh, live dangerously, Beaudin," she said and laughed.

Amersen pushed back his chair and stood, moving around the table. He took her hand and silently asked her permission to draw her gently to her feet, pulling her close. Then he grasped her chin and tilted her head back.

"Is this dangerous enough?" he asked, feeling every inch of her pressed against him. He was half-aroused and not afraid to let her know it. Because he would never take any more than she was prepared to give willingly. And she knew that about him—he was certain of it. Her gaze was slumberous and tempting, her cheeks tinged pink, her mouth slightly parted, inviting his kiss. He moved closer, dipping his head to reach her lips, feeling her sigh like a breath as he angled his mouth over hers. Her hands moved around him, resting on his hips for a moment before she slid them up his back. Her lips tasted like chocolate, and he suddenly decided he did like sweets. When she thrust her tongue into his mouth, sensation arrowed directly to his groin.

He could have taken her there and then. He could have lifted her up and carried her to the counter, stripped off her jeans and panties, and plunged inside her, feeling her slick and tight around him, seeking the sensual oblivion he craved. But he wanted more than some quick, mindless release. He wanted to tease her, taste her, feel every inch of her skin with his mouth and hands. He wanted to watch her come apart beneath him. He wanted to be inside her, to feel her shudder, to absorb every pulse of pleasure as she reached orgasm. And he wanted to make her forget every other man she'd known.

"You can't stay," she moaned against his mouth. "You just can't."

"I know," he muttered.

"Go," she said, still kissing him. "Go…before I change my mind."

Leaving her a few minutes later was one of the hardest things he'd ever done. He yearned. He craved. He ached. And he knew she felt exactly the same way.

Amersen also knew that being *just friends* with Robin Harbin was totally out of the question.

Chapter Seven

By the time breakfast was done the next morning and they were back walking down East Sixth Street, it was close to 11:00 a.m. Robin had always enjoyed exploring the city, and having Amersen for company made the experience richer than she dared think about.

The night before, she'd been so close to asking him to stay and make love to her. Somehow, she'd come to her senses. *Just.* Making him leave was like slicing open her heart and denying her body what it craved most. She'd never experienced such rampant, overwhelming desire for anyone before. Not her high school boyfriend. And certainly not Trey. By comparison, her feelings for both other men had been lukewarm at best. But Amersen evoked passion she hadn't known she possessed. It was like he had tapped into a part of her and awakened sexual desire and longing.

"What are you thinking about?"

Amersen's voice jerked her back into the present. She certainly wasn't going to admit she'd been thinking about how good it would be to have sex with him!

"Shopping," she said and smiled, feeling a shot of electricity strike up her arm as their fingers accidentally touched. "We have to get that key ring, remember? I need to get something for Kate and Sterling for

Christmas. And Otis, my right-hand man at the ranch. You can help me choose."

He nodded. "Lead the way."

In worn jeans that she suspected cost a fortune, a blue sweater and his leather jacket, he looked effortlessly masculine. He had a long black scarf around his neck that looked like it cost more than she earned in a week and did nothing to lessen the purely alpha male picture he evoked. His hair was mussed in its usual sexy style, his jaw had a sexy stubble that was too damned arousing for words and he smelled so good she could barely stand being more than six inches from his side. Just being around him was an aphrodisiac. And the more time they spent together, the more she wanted to share his company.

Which meant she was in for one hell of a ride.

And then a major fall.

They found their way to Second Street and browsed through several boutiques, where she found a lovely silk scarf for Kate. It was a modest purchase, but she still refused his offer to buy it for her. Money had never impressed Robin in the past, and she wasn't going to change her view on that score. At a secondhand bookstore an hour later, she found a leather-bound edition of *Gulliver's Travels* that Amersen suggested would be a thoughtful gift for Sterling. In a tourist shop he bought a few mementos for his family, including a baseball cap for his father. Then they spent a couple of hours comparing the Christmas windows at some of the more enthusiastic shops and boutiques in the neighborhood. By two o'clock they'd had lunch at a bistro, then by four thirty had moved on to drinks at a hip place on Ninth Street and later listened to a grunge band playing '70s rock covers.

And not once did either of them mention their aborted make-out session the night before.

But Robin wasn't fooled. They might not have ended up in bed together, but the sex was there between them, waving like a great red flag. She couldn't believe that *not* having sex had become as complicated as if they'd dived between the sheets for a few hours.

Instead, they talked. About anything and everything. She discovered that they liked much of the same music and had a proclivity for old movies. They talked politics and religion, economics and social media, and fashion and food. He told her about his wine brand and his ambitious plans to have it served at all the finest restaurants around the world. She told him of her dream of using her degree in plant biology as a stepping-stone for further research into natural remedies for some chronic ailments. He listened as she spoke, offering the occasional word of advice and counsel, but mostly he was interested and attentive, and as the day progressed, Robin felt as though they had more in common than not.

He was, she realized, perfect boyfriend material.

Even if, she suspected, he'd never considered himself right for the role with any woman. He was clearly a serial monogamist. He never cheated. Never dated more than one woman at a time. But he never made a commitment longer than a month, either. He opened up about his family and she learned he had a close relationship with his mother; when he showed her a picture, Robin was taken aback by the still young and still beautiful woman who had given birth to him twenty-five years earlier. Suzette Beaudin was forty-five but looked a decade younger, and her handsome husband was eight years her senior. A big contrast to Robin's own parents, since Veronica had her first child at twenty-eight and her last ten years later.

"My dad was forty when I was born," Robin said, sipping the wine she'd ordered at the obscure little bar a few doors down from the bistro. "So my parents have always seemed, you know, *oldish.*"

"Your father was there," Amersen said quietly. "That's all that matters, isn't it?"

"Of course," she replied, realizing how ungrateful she must have sounded. "I didn't mean I wasn't… I'm sorry if that made you think about…you know…your…"

"Sperm donor?"

Her expression narrowed. "Why do you call him that?"

"It's what he is," Amersen replied, watching her over the rim of his glass. "Just a moment of failed contraception."

She wanted to reach out and grasp his hand but didn't. "It hurts you, though."

He shrugged. "No. That would mean I cared. And I don't."

Robin wasn't sure she believed him. "What if he tried to find you? Would you be—"

"Let's go dancing," he said and pushed his chair back, cutting off the rest of her words.

She looked toward the street. It was nearly dark and the streets were busy with pedestrians and a steady flow of traffic. Robin looked down at her jeans, crumpled blouse and jacket, and purple boots. She really wasn't dressed for a nightclub. And foolishly, she didn't want to share Amersen with a whole room full of onlookers, particularly any interested women who might circle around him.

Maybe they were just friends who happen to make

out every now and then, but that didn't mean she wanted him on the open market while they were out together.

"I have a better idea," she said and got to her feet.

"Where are we going?" Amersen asked.

"You'll see."

It was an old theatre, he discovered some time later as he pulled up in the parking area and parked the rental car.

And it was busy with people. Old people, young people, families…all filing in through the wide doors.

They got out of the car and she waited until he was by her side, then grasped his hand and smiled. "You ready for this?"

He smiled and allowed her to lead him toward the entrance. "So, we're at the movies?"

"It's A Wonderful Life," she explained, grinning. "They play it here every Saturday and Sunday night in the lead-up to Christmas. It's my favorite Christmas movie."

He wasn't surprised. She looked delighted by the idea, and seeing her so happy did something to him inside. All day he'd had a strange feeling in the center of his chest. Sure, there was an undercurrent of attraction and desire between them—but this was something else. Something that had nothing to do with sex and everything to do with the fact that he couldn't remember the last time he'd had such a calm, enjoyable day.

Never.

Because he'd never spent a day with anyone as intoxicating and lovely as Robin.

"Is this okay?" she asked, clearly sensing his surprise.

Amersen nodded. "Sure. Great."

They waited in line for a few minutes to purchase tickets and were quickly ushered up to the theater. The place was old but had obviously gone through a recent renovation.

"It was going to be demolished," she said, as though reading his thoughts. "But the local historical society fought the plans and took the developers to court, and thankfully the place was listed on the historical buildings register. They had a good lawyer," she said and grinned. "My brother Reece does a lot of pro bono work. And he's something of a tree hugger and wasn't going to allow this beautiful building to be pulled down."

The pride and admiration in her voice couldn't be denied. He liked how close she was to her family and it made him miss his own more than he'd believed possible. But he was also torn, knowing that he would miss Robin once he returned home.

They found seats at the rear of the theater, up high and with a great view of the screen. When she shivered, he pulled off his scarf and draped it around her neck, shushing her as she protested.

"Be back in a minute," he said with a grin.

He headed back out to the foyer, and when he returned with a hot chocolate for her and a small bag of warm doughnuts, she groaned her approval. He sat down and passed her the drink.

"I know I shouldn't be hungry, since we've pretty much been grazing all day, but this was a great idea," she said and waved a sugared doughnut. "Want a bite?"

There was innuendo and flirtation in her words, and Amersen met her seductive gaze, saying nothing.

"No?" she queried.

He chuckled. "I don't eat sweets."

Her eyes widened, and then she frowned. "But last night you—"

"An aberration," he said and drank his black coffee.

She looked indignant for a moment and then laughed. "Good...more for me. Although if I keep eating at this rate, I'll put on ten pounds before the weekend is over."

Amersen looked straight ahead at the blank movie screen. "You have a very sexy body, Robin. Ten pounds wouldn't change that."

She sighed, then grabbed his hand and laid it on her thigh. "You know, you could probably read a phone book to me, and with your accent, it would be the most erotic thing I've ever heard." She nibbled on the doughnut. "My friend Francesca reckons that her English husband has the sexy-accent thing going, but I don't know. I think the French accent is more...seductive. Next time I see Francesca and Keaton, I'll have to compare."

Caution rose up his spine and Amersen stilled instantly. "You mean Keaton Whitfield?"

She nodded. "Yeah, I think he uses both Whitfield and Fortune now. He's one of those illegitimate Fortunes. Seems like one pops up every now and then."

Amersen swallowed the rising panic in his throat. His breath felt heavy in his chest, but thankfully he had an inhaler in his pocket if the need arose.

"You said you knew his wife?" he asked, his chest tight, remembering how her parents had spoken about knowing several of Gerald Robinson's illegitimate children.

"We went to college together. We don't hang out much now or anything because we're both so busy, but we catch up for coffee every couple of months." She sipped her hot chocolate. "Do you know Keaton?"

"We've never met," Amersen replied, thinking it

wasn't exactly a lie. He had never met his half sibling in person. Every communication from the other man or Ben Fortune Robinson had been via email—until the note he'd left at the hotel the other night. Perhaps Robin had mentioned to Whitfield's wife that Amersen was in town… Whatever the circumstance, it was all seeming a little too close for comfort.

The movie credits started, and Amersen heaved a relieved sigh. He didn't want to think about anything other than enjoying the remainder of the evening. Robin's attention was immediately taken up with the movie, and over the course of the following couple of hours, he watched as she sighed, laughed and cried as she absorbed the movie and its whole sappy nonsense. She edged closer to him as the film progressed, and by the time the end came, her head was tucked neatly against his shoulder, their thighs pressed intimately together. As people started moving to leave the theater, Amersen heard her stifle a yawn.

"Come on, *tu dors debout*," he said, getting to his feet as he translated. "Sleepyhead. Time for me to get you home."

She nodded, and they quickly packed up their belongings and headed back to the car.

The drive back to her ranch was quiet, with a tinge of regret in the air, as though they both knew their day together was coming to an end. If she invited him in, he knew they would make love. It was inevitable.

But she didn't.

He walked her to her door, noticed that a light flicked on in the main house, and then he waited while she unlocked the screen. "So, good night," he said and passed her the shopping bags.

"Good night, Amersen. Thank you for a lovely day."

He wanted to kiss her so much that his mouth tingled and his gut burned. "I had a nice time today."

"Me, too," she admitted. "So, kiss me good-night and go back to your hotel."

"Good night," he said, drawing on every ounce of his self-control to press his lips to her cheek and not ravage her mouth with his own.

"I'll see you Monday," she said quietly, stepping back.

He'd already explained that his flight left Monday afternoon and that he would be stopping by Sterling's Fortune to see Kate before he flew out of Austin. "If you would like to have dinner tomorrow night, I will be at the hotel. Say, around six?"

"No."

He frowned. "No?"

"Every time I say good-night to you, it's harder, if you get my meaning."

Amersen understood. Even if he didn't like the idea. "So, this is it? Our last time together as friends?"

She nodded. "Yes. Absolutely."

He kissed her cheek again, stepped back and dropped his arms. "Then *bonne nuit*, Robin."

And by the time he got back to his car, she was already inside her house and the door was closed.

On Sunday morning, Robin took Butterfly out for a long ride. It was chilly and overcast, and by the time she returned to the stables, it was spitting rain. She spotted her brother's Jeep in the driveway and smiled. Both her brothers knew their parents would be at church this morning, so he'd obviously come to visit her. Reece was always good to talk to, a little more serious than Evan, but less disapproving. And she needed someone to talk to about Amersen. She wished she had a girl-friend close at hand to spill her woes to, but her best friend, Amy, was traveling through South America with her boyfriend and wouldn't be back in Austin for several weeks. Other than Amy, she had a few other female friends she could call, but she didn't feel like explaining how she felt when she could barely explain her feelings to herself. But Reece would have an understanding ear.

Only, when she dismounted, grabbed Butterfly's reins and walked into the stables, it wasn't Reece sitting on a hay bale waiting for her. It was Evan.

"Where's the Bimmer?" she asked and tied Butterfly to a hitch.

He grimaced. "Fender bender last night. And Reece is in Dallas on business, so I borrowed his car until I pick up a rental this afternoon."

She nodded and loosened the cinch. "The folks won't be back for another couple of hours. Mom's got that quilting class after church."

"I know," he said and wandered toward her. "How was your date yesterday?"

Her fingers fumbled. "My date?"

"I saw you in town," he replied. "With Beaudin."

"Spying on me now?"

"Coincidence," he said, pulling the saddle off Butterfly. "I was out and saw you from across the street. You looked…happy."

"Something wrong with that?" she asked.

Evan scowled. "Don't get all loco on me. I'm just concerned."

"We had this conversation the other day," she reminded him and grabbed a currycomb from the bucket by the stall.

"And yet you didn't take my advice."

"Oh," she said with emphasis. "That was *advice*? I thought it was you being a bossy older brother and telling me how to live my life."

"I'm not gonna apologize for being concerned about you."

Irritated, Robin turned and glared at him. "What exactly do you think Amersen is going to do, Evan?"

"Break your heart," he said flatly.

"My heart is fine," she assured him. "We're friends, that's all. And he's leaving tomorrow, so you have nothing more to worry about."

"Good," he said. "I'm glad. I don't like him."

She made an exasperated sound. "You're such an idiot. You don't know him."

"And you do?"

"Yes," she said hotly. "I do. He's not what you think. And this conversation is over. Again."

"Why are you being so stubborn about this, Rob?" he asked, using the shortened version of her name as he'd done since she was a child. "The guy is bad news, and it looks like you're the only one who can't see it."

Robin's temper kindled. "How about you sort out your own love life before you start interfering in mine."

Her brother threw his hands up in the air. "What? You're in love with him now?"

She let out an exasperated sigh. "That's not what I said. I *like* him, okay. That's all. We're the same age, we like a lot of the same things, he's interesting and smart and easy on the eyes. Not that I have to explain myself to you or anyone else. *I like Amersen Beaudin!*" she exclaimed and ran the brush over Butterfly's neck. "There…I said it. I like him and he likes me. We're adults, so it's allowed. I don't need to ask your permission to like him, to see him or to even have crazy wild sex with him if I want to. So, just mind your own damn business already!"

Evan look predictably uncomfortable at the idea of his baby sister doing any such thing. But she was tired of the interference, tired of being told what to do. It wasn't as though Amersen was some kind of ogre taking advantage of her. In fact, he'd been nothing but respectful and considerate. Her family, and Evan in particular, were out of line.

"I'm only trying to—"

"You're trying to control me," she cut him off. "And I won't stand for it, Evan. I didn't see all this concern when Trey was cheating on me with—"

"I didn't want to hurt you," he said quickly and then clammed up when he realized what he'd said.

Robin's gaze narrowed tightly. "You knew?"

He shrugged. "I…I…"

"You knew he was cheating and you didn't tell me?" she demanded as betrayal seeped through her blood and into her bones. "How could you?"

"I was trying to protect you," he said quickly. "We both were."

Her suspicions soared. "Reece knew, too?"

Evan nodded. "We were out one night at that new honky-tonk place off the highway," he explained and let out a long breath. "We saw him there, with this girl, and it looked…well, I guess you know how it looked. Afterward, we thought it best not to say anything. We talked to Trey…he said it was a onetime thing. Reece threatened to knock his teeth out if he did it again, and we really thought he would come to his senses and stop behaving like such an ass."

"He didn't."

He shrugged again. "I know, I'm sorry."

"Me, too," she said, feeling so hurt she could barely breathe. "It would have been easier *hearing* it from you than *seeing* it with my own eyes. Go home, Evan. I'll tell the folks you dropped by."

Long after her brother left, Robin was still in the stables, brushing Butterfly and thinking about how she was so coddled by her family that her brothers thought it was okay to lie to her about the man she'd believed she would marry one day. But it wasn't okay. It was brutal. It was gut-wrenching.

Since she'd caught Trey cheating in such a humiliating way, Robin had become a hermit, staying home, refusing invitations to go out, saying no to anything that would make her seem available. Because she was hurt and betrayed and had lost faith in people. In men. And now even her brothers had proved her right. She used to enjoy parties and company and socializing…now her weekly highlight was having dinner with her parents.

Until Amersen.

Somehow, he'd helped heal the bridge between her humiliation and despair.

I like him and he likes me.

The words she'd said to her brother earlier stayed with her. Because it was that simple. She liked him. She wanted him.

It was chemistry, pure and simple.

And suddenly, it was enough.

She didn't want to waste another moment thinking about how he was leaving the next day. So…he'd come back. Or he wouldn't. It would work out, or it wouldn't. They didn't have to make grand statements or demand commitment. They were both young and single. And the shackles of the past few months, the ones that had been holding her back from enjoying herself and actually having a life, suddenly fell to her feet. Because she knew what she wanted. And she'd go and get it. Right now. Because if she didn't, she sensed she would regret it for the rest of her life.

Fueled by bravado, later that afternoon Robin showered, applied makeup and dressed in her favorite purple crushed-velvet dress that showed off a good portion of her neckline and hugged under her bust, emphasizing her waist and curvy hips. She wore heels, the kind that were good for only short distances, grabbed her bag and by six o'clock was heading into Austin.

The hotel where Amersen was staying was the best in town. A valet greeted her as she pulled up outside, and she ignored the tremble in her knees as she headed toward the lobby. The place was busy, bustling with guests and staff, and Robin took a few long breaths. She had never done this before—she'd never actively pursued a man in her life. And now here she was, standing in a hotel lobby, dressed for sex, and suddenly she realized that she might have overplayed her hand. She didn't even know if he was at the hotel. What if he was out? Perhaps he had a date? A man who looked like Amersen wouldn't have to try hard to find company. She might have walked right into another humiliating scene, and it would be like catching Trey with his pants around his ankles all over again. A sensible woman would have called first.

A sensible woman wouldn't have sent him away night after night.

Robin pulled her cell from her bag, found his number and quickly sent a text before she lost her nerve.

I'm downstairs.

And she waited. Two minutes later her cell pinged.

Don't move.

She couldn't have moved if she tried. Her legs were wobbling so much she thought she'd fall if she dared take a step. And then, minutes later, she saw him, striding toward her from the elevator. Dressed in black, he looked handsome and exotic and exactly what she craved to quell the desire thrumming through her body. He stopped a few feet away, his gaze traveling over her slowly, until finally he reached her eyes.

"Hi," she said.

"Hello," he said, his voice raspy. "I didn't expect to see you tonight."

Robin shrugged one shoulder. "I know. I'm sorry, I should have called first. I was... I was..."

"You look so beautiful," he said, the rawness in his tone speaking volumes.

Robin fiddled with the edge of her dress. "It's... purple."

"It's... *jolie*," he said. "Lovely."

She swallowed hard. "I was wondering if you still wanted to—"

"Yes," he said quickly, cutting her off. "Of course."

She smiled. He was nervous. She liked that. It relaxed her edgy nerves. "I thought we could have dinner if you still wanted to...unless you have other plans."

"I have no other plans," he said and reached out to grasp her hand and then gently pull her close. He leaned in and kissed her cheek. *"Mon Dieu,"* he muttered against her neck. "You take my breath away."

Robin's weakened knees trembled. "Amersen." She

said his name on a sigh and then gently touched his jaw with her fingertips. "Would you do something for me?"

He grabbed her hand, looked directly into her eyes and pressed her knuckles to his mouth. "Anything."

"Would you make love to me tonight?"

He groaned out her name, gently squeezing her fingers. "I'll give you a night you will never forget."

Chapter Eight

He was nervous. Watching Robin walking around the luxurious hotel suite, her fingertips caressing the back of the sofa, the table, the balustrade leading out to the patio—it turned his usual confidence to mush.

He ordered dinner, agreeing with her suggestion that they eat in his suite. He wanted to have as much alone time with her as he could. He opened a bottle of wine, a pinot noir from his own vineyard that he'd brought with him, and he watched as she took a sip, mesmerized by the way she savored the taste. She did everything with such intense passion—she tended the gardens at the Fortune ranch with a zeal and commitment that was riveting. She rode a horse as though she'd been born in the saddle; she ate a doughnut as though it were a delicate pastry; she spoke about Christmas with animated delight. And she kissed with a hunger that undid him.

Knowing they were going to make love, knowing he would be touching her, kissing her, making her his own in the most intimate way possible, filled the air between them with a kind of blistering-hot awareness.

"This is nice," she said and gestured to the glass in her hand.

"It is from my vineyard," he explained, so aroused

by the mere sight of her that he could barely stand being in his own skin.

She smiled. "Tell me about it."

"It is on a hill in the Loire Valley. It has a house on it that I am planning to renovate. There is much to do, as the home has not been lived in for many years, but it has the most spectacular view of the vines. In the evenings, the sun sets and the colors mix with the scents of lavender and rosemary that are embedded deep within the earth."

Her gaze was locked with his. "It sounds magical."

"It is," he said softly. "One day, I think I would very much like to live there."

She had a tiny smile on her lips. "So, maybe you're not such a nightlife-loving playboy after all."

He couldn't help shrugging. "Maybe. I don't know… I think perhaps I just live the life I have and don't let myself believe I have time for anything else. But the vineyard…" His voice trailed off for a moment. "It is away from the city, away from the world. I can imagine what it might be like to simply sit out on the balcony with a glass of wine as the sun sets." He met her gaze straight on. "I would like it very much if you would visit sometime."

"I'd like that, too."

His heart surged, and for the first time in his life Amersen wondered if what he was feeling was more than simply physical desire. Because the idea of having her beside him at his home on the hill didn't make him want to run a mile. He'd never sought commitment in a relationship; he'd never dated anyone long enough to recognize any woman as his *petite amie*…a girlfriend. Lover, certainly…but a girlfriend was different. But Robin made him think about it. Being with her was easy. It felt…right. As though they'd known each other forever and not a matter of mere days.

There was a knock on the door, and his thoughts were quickly diverted. "Our dinner."

Within minutes they had their meal on the table by the balcony, their wineglasses were refilled and the waiter who had brought the food discreetly disappeared. Amersen pulled out a chair and beckoned Robin to sit. Once she was in the chair, he lingered behind her for a moment, noticing her beautiful neck and how her long hair hung down her back. Never in his life had he met a woman with such beautiful hair.

"I have something for you," he said as he sat and passed her a small box that was on the table. "I meant to give this to you tomorrow, before I left."

She took the box and met his gaze levelly. "Another gift?"

He shrugged, faintly embarrassed. "It is just a—"

"As much as I appreciate the gesture," she said softly and laid her hand over his, "I don't need gifts. That's not why I'm here with you, Amersen. I know you're wealthy, and maybe in the past you've known women who want something from you that comes in a box… but I don't. I don't care about your money or your fame. I don't care that you have countless followers on your social media accounts and that every move you make is probably watched with interest by the paparazzi. That person," she said with a kind of raspy emphasis, "that man, the one who owns a nightclub and knows celebrities by their first names and writes a blog that's read by millions of people around the world…that's not the man I want to be with tonight." She rubbed her thumb gently across his knuckles. "The man I want to be with is the one who makes me laugh, the one who looks at me and makes me feel like I'm the only woman in the room. You," she said softly. "Just you."

His chest inexplicably tightened. "I can take the gift back to the store if you—"

"Just be yourself," she said warmly and patted his hand. "That's all I want."

"I guess I am not good at this…thing?"

Her mouth curled at the edges. "What thing?"

He searched for the right word. "I don't know…this dating thing."

She smiled broadly. "Is that what we're doing?"

He shrugged. "I have no real idea. I did not come to Austin expecting to meet someone like you. And the gift…" He paused, taking a breath, feeling the heat of her stare through to his soul. "The gift is merely a clumsy way of saying what I cannot say with words."

She gasped slightly and pulled her hand away. Her eyes were never bluer and glittered brilliantly. He watched as she unwrapped the box and held the trinket in her hand. He'd found the jeweled unicorn, attached to a gold linked chain, days earlier and had instantly thought of Robin.

"It's beautiful," she said and met his gaze. "Thank you."

He nodded slightly. "My pleasure."

She smiled and then began eating. Amersen wasn't particularly hungry, but he ate a little, and when she was done with her meal, he offered her a selection from the desserts he'd ordered. She tried a little of both the tiramisu and the chocolate-orange mousse, and he watched as she licked the spoon, rolling her eyes back delightedly.

"God, that is divine," she said and caressed the mousse in her mouth with her tongue in a motion that was so damned erotic he went hard instantly. "Better than sex."

Amersen had every intention of proving her wrong. "Want to bet?"

She laughed loudly, and her tongue danced over her lower lip. Without another word, she pushed back her chair and stood, had a sip of wine and then held out her hand. "Mr. Beaudin, I believe you promised me a night I wouldn't forget."

"That I did," he said and took her hand.

The bedroom was as luxurious as the rest of the suite, but Amersen only noticed Robin. He flicked on the bedside lamp, keeping their fingers linked. Her creamy skin was like a beacon, and he fought the overwhelming urge to trace his tongue along her collarbone. He wanted to touch her so much he ached; he wanted to find out what she liked, to kiss her deeply and hear her moans and then hear her plead and whisper his name over and over.

Doucement...doucement, Beaudin...slowly.

"Are you okay?" she asked, watching him intently.

Amersen urged her toward him. "Fine. You?"

She nodded. "Kiss me," she begged. "Kiss me before I wake up from this dream."

"It's not a dream," he promised and hovered his mouth above hers. "I'm here. You're here."

He captured her mouth, drawing her closer, feeling her lovely curves pressed against him. Her tongue was quickly wrapped around his, her breath shallow, her hands on his back. Amersen changed angles, moving his mouth across hers, going deeper, hotter, wetter, until he had to take a long, shuddering breath. He kissed her jaw and then the spot below her ear where a pulse beckoned. He molded his hands over her shoulders and down her arms, then threaded them around her waist. She searched for his lips again, taking his tongue deep in her mouth. He anchored a hand at her nape, spreading fingers through her silky hair, going even deeper into her sweet mouth. And he was consumed...by heat and desire and the knowledge that he wanted her like he'd never wanted a woman before.

He lifted his head, watched as she sucked in air as though it pained her, and met her gaze. Then she pulled back, chest heaving, her lips reddened from his kiss. And she looked like some kind of exotic goddess, with her mussed-up hair and slightly swollen mouth. Amersen kept his gaze locked with hers, his entire body rigid, watching in a kind of lustful agony as she undid the zipper on her dress and slowly let the velvet garment drop to her feet. In a lilac lace bra and thong and her killer heels, she was all smooth curves, her beautiful skin dappled in the lamplight. If she had any imperfections, he didn't notice them. She was pure beauty. And for the next few hours, she was his.

He took her hand and led her to the bed, gently easing her back against the covers. And he kissed her again, and again. Deep, hot kisses that made him harder than he believed possible. But he wasn't going to rush anything. He was going to love her right. He wanted to pleasure her, to feel her writhe, to watch her skin flush, to taste and touch every part of her.

Her hands were in his hair as he trailed his mouth down her jaw and neck and lower, to her breasts, which were fuller than he'd dared allow himself to imagine. The bra clipped at the front, and he flicked it open with one deft move. He heard her delighted chuckle, and then she arched her back as he took one straining rosy nipple into his mouth. It pebbled against his tongue, sending a shot of arousal to his groin that was so acute it was almost painful.

Then he went lower, kissing her rib cage and belly, gently kneading her breasts with his hands as his mouth trailed down her stomach and farther, until finally he was between her thighs. He dragged the thong aside and kissed her intimately, finding the spot that would give her the most pleasure. She almost bucked off the bed, but he held her hips firm, caressing her with his mouth, finding the tiny nub and gently rolling her clitoris with his tongue. Within minutes she came apart, moaning loudly as she climaxed, and Amersen experienced a deep surge of gratification that consumed him to his very soul.

She was panting, drawing in long breaths, her hand across her face. "Oh, I was wrong."

He moved, getting to his knees, looking at her. "Wrong?"

She moved her hand from her face and met his gaze. "That is so much better than chocolate."

He grinned. "Told you so."

She shifted onto her elbows and looked him over. "Are you going to take off your clothes anytime soon?"

Amersen glanced down. He was still fully dressed, while she was naked except for her thong. He looked at her breasts, noticing that her nipples were hard, and her skin still glowed with the flush of her climax. She was easily the most beautiful thing he had ever seen. And then he had his clothes off in about three seconds flat.

"Now," she said, smiling seductively as she crooked a finger, beckoning him. "My turn."

Not that she had a lot of experience for comparison, but he was big. That was the first thing Robin noticed as Amersen ditched his clothes like a man possessed. The second thing she noticed was that he had a perfectly sculptured physique—smooth tanned skin, broad shoulders, a flat washboard belly and a Celtic tattoo circling one bicep. And she managed to notice it all while she was still pulsating from experiencing the most torturously intense orgasm of her life.

And then all she could think about was how she wanted more of him.

All of him.

By the time he was back on the bed, he'd dragged her thong down her thighs and was kissing her hotly— mindless, drugging kisses that made her abandon all coherent thought. His hands were all over her, over her shoulders, down her back, her behind, between her legs. He teased and caressed; he urged and encouraged. He was, she realized as she came again some minutes later, the most utterly unselfish and astonishing lover she had ever had.

And the more they touched, the more she learned. She discovered she could make him tremble by kissing his neck. She could make him moan by tracing her tongue over his navel. When she took his hard length in her hand, he offered words of encouragement that might have shocked her, but his sexy accent was like a potent aphrodisiac and drove her to do more. There was nothing particularly practiced or skilled about her technique, just an eagerness to please, and that was obviously enough. She touched him freely, with her hands, with her mouth, making him crazy, making him laugh, making him moan.

That was what stunned her the most. Not the erotic heat. Not the mind-blowing pleasure. But the way they were completely in tune with each other. There was no awkwardness, no reserve. Just complete and unabashed trust.

"Robin," he pleaded, his voice an agonized whisper. "I can't take any more."

Robin looked at him, her hair draped over his chest. His expression spoke volumes and she experienced a delightful sense of satisfaction. Without another word, she grabbed the foil packet on the bedside table and handed it to him.

He sheathed himself and then settled between her legs, nudging her entrance. Robin knew she was ready for him, and then finally he was inside her. She looked up, matched his gaze and barely blinked as he began to move. Nothing could have prepared her for the sensations he evoked.

Then he kissed her, their tongues dancing together as he created a slow, steady rhythm. He made love like he did everything—with hunger and confidence. And then he changed positions, rolling them over until she straddled him, and he held her hips, moving her back and forth in a way that was sinfully arousing. By the time release claimed them, he was back on top, driving into her with so much passion and intensity she could barely contain the scream of pleasure that formed in her throat. He kissed her as he shuddered, smothering her moans, making her mindless—and making her more connected to him than she ever had been to another person in her entire life.

When he rolled off her, he was breathing hard, his chest rising up and down. Robin's whole body was pulsing from the aftermath, every cell super sensitive.

"I think I am lucky I did not have a heart attack," he said in between heavy breaths.

She chuckled and closed her eyes. "Yeah, but what a way to go."

She heard laughter rumble in his chest. "True."

"And you're in pretty good condition." She trailed her fingers along his side, delighted to find he was ticklish. "You're probably one of those annoying people who've never been ill in their life."

"Wrong," he said, eyes still closed. "I was a sickly child. Asthma," he explained and pointed to the inhaler on the bedside table. "It still gets me occasionally."

Robin rolled onto her side. "I think I like you more knowing you're not completely perfect."

He laughed again and then excused himself for a moment to go to the bathroom to dispose of the condom. When he returned, he flopped back onto the bed heavily, sliding beneath the covers.

"That was really great sex," she said, smiling as she peeked sideways.

His eyes were shut. "Yes," he agreed, laughing softly. "You are a noisy lover. I expect a complaint any moment from the concierge."

"Ha!" she said and tossed a pillow in his direction. "All your fault."

He was smirking. "I am happy to take the blame. It is good for my ego."

"I don't think your ego needs any inflating," she remarked as her hand made its way beneath the covers and worked its way along his thigh. "But if you need something else inflated…"

He laughed and rolled, pinning her beneath him. "Insatiable woman."

She chuckled. "I've decided I'm going to give up chocolate and just do this instead."

"Good idea." He kissed her and then looked a little

solemn. "Robin…why did you change your mind about this? Yesterday you said—"

"I know what I said," she cut him off. "I changed my mind because the truth is I was mad at myself for not taking what I wanted. Life is too short. And then after what Evan said, I just—"

"Evan?"

She shrugged lightly and traced a finger along his jaw. "I found out today that both my brothers knew my ex had been cheating. They had caught him red-handed and never breathed a word to me. I'm sure they would have let me get engaged and then get married." She made an irritated sound. "I felt betrayed and angry."

He looked serious. "Perhaps they were simply trying to protect you?"

"By lying to me?" She shook her head. "That's not protection. That's them trying to control my life. Anyway, it doesn't matter now."

"It does if you're here because you wanted a little revenge or are trying to prove a point."

She scowled. "That's not why I'm here, I assure you."

He kissed her again, and she felt his growing arousal pressed against her. "Glad to hear it," he whispered as he trailed his mouth down her neck.

They made love again, hotter, wilder, with more laughter and passion and a kind of easy companionship. The more they touched, the more they kissed and caressed, the more Robin felt herself falling. Hard. Because as the night turned into morning, she knew she had feelings for Amersen that were beyond physical attraction.

Way beyond.

She'd never imagined she would fall in love with him. Lust, yes. But not in love with a man she hardly knew. And yet, on so many levels, she felt as though she knew him, and that he knew her, better than anyone.

Afterward, they slept, legs entwined, hands linked. When she woke up, there was a tiny sliver of light peeking through the side of the heavy blinds, and she rolled over to avoid getting morning sun in her eyes. Amersen lay on his stomach, one arm flung out over the edge of the bed, his dark hair a stark contrast against the white pillowcase. The sheet was draped low, exposing his back and hips. His smooth skin was so inviting her fingers itched with the need to touch him. She noticed a mark on his shoulder blade and another at his ribs. Love bites. Symbols of possession and passion. She probably had a few herself. She ached in places she'd forgotten could ache—but it was a heady, evocative kind of feeling. He was undeniably skilled in the bedroom and had brought her to the peak of pleasure several times. He brought out her wild side, the passionate part of her nature that she'd kept under wraps for too long. Her passion…and her heart.

Robin sucked in a long breath, feeling like such a fraud. Her great plans the night before—about taking what she wanted and not living with regret—those plans now seemed to be laughing in her face. Her insides were inexplicably tight, her breath sharp and painful, and as she looked at him, she was desperate to touch him but also unwilling to wake him up. If she did, they would make love again. And she wasn't sure she could bear it.

Wanting him was one thing. Having real feelings for him—*loving him*—that was another thing altogether. Because he didn't feel the same. He'd wooed her, he'd pursued her for days with his sexy voice and undivided attention…but she was savvy enough to know it was all part of the endgame. For this. For a night of hot sex and fun. Amersen Beaudin didn't do relationships…he'd already made that abundantly clear. He hadn't said he was staying in Austin any longer than planned. He hadn't made any promises. He'd been himself, and she'd fallen for his smooth line of seduction like any woman would.

But she wasn't about to let him see she wanted it to be any more than that.

She shimmied off the bed and looked around for her clothes. She found her shoes, her bra and her dress and quietly put them on in that order. Her thong was harder to find, but she eventually spotted it at the bottom of the bed, twisted up in the sheets. He stirred and she stilled instantly, caught like a rabbit in headlights.

He groaned and rolled, exposing way more of himself than was good for her libido. She dragged her eyes away and pulled on the thong.

"Bonjour," he said raspily and turned onto his side, taking some of the sheet with him. He looked her over, a sexy smile curling his mouth. "You are dressed?"

Robin nodded. "I have to go," she said quickly. "I need to get home to change and then go to work."

He frowned. "Work?"

"It's Monday," she reminded him, silently wishing he would stop looking so damned gorgeous. "And I have to get to Sterling's Fortune." She paused, sucking in breath and bravado. "But maybe I'll see you there later. I imagine you want to say goodbye to Kate before your flight this afternoon."

He was still frowning. "You're leaving? Now?"

Robin nodded again. "Yes. So, thanks for a great evening. I'll never forget it." She pushed some strength into her legs and walked around the bed. Determined to stay strong and resilient, she bent down and gave him a quick kiss on the cheek, then straightened and smiled broadly. "It's been a lot of fun, Amersen. Goodbye."

Before he could respond, she turned and walked from the room, detouring to the sofa to collect her bag before she left the suite, closing the door behind her. Once she was out in the hall, she backed up against the door, knees like Jell-O.

It's better this way...

Better that she made the first move to leave before she had a chance to forget good sense and beg him not to return to Paris. It was over. Done.

And as she strode down the hallway and toward the elevator, Robin wiped tears from her eyes and realized two indisputable facts—she was in love with Amersen Beaudin. And she'd pretty much sent him packing!

Blown off.

Amersen didn't like how it felt. Not one bit. He wasn't used to it. Usually, he was the one who bailed first. No, not usually. *Always.* He always left before things got awkward. Sex without consequence. Without strings or expectations. Simple and satisfying. He'd been doing that for years, and not once had a woman ever made the first move to leave.

Until now.

He sat up and swung his legs off the bed, inhaling heavily and still imagining he could pick up the scent of her perfume in the room. Hell, he wasn't even sure it was perfume. It could have been simply soap or shampoo. She was that kind of woman—no frills or fakeness. Honest. Playful. And too damned beautiful for his peace of mind.

Amersen headed for the bathroom and took a shower, trying—and failing—to wash the intoxicating scent of her from his skin. He dressed, ordered breakfast, packed his things and then called the concierge and arranged for his rental car to be returned and a limo to take him to Sterling's Fortune.

By the end of his second cup of coffee, he was no closer to understanding why she'd left. The night had been good. Better than good. They were insanely great together in bed. It had been the hottest and most satisfying sex of his life, and he arrogantly assumed she didn't have any complaints about his performance.

Maybe he was wrong?

He picked up the unicorn necklace she'd left on the table.

The man I want to be with is the one who makes me laugh, the one who looks at me and makes me feel like I'm the only woman in the room. You. Just you.

Her words banged around in his head. Foolishly, a part of him wanted to believe them. And the more he considered how she'd left in such a hurry, the more irritated and resentful he became.

No one bailed on Amersen Beaudin.

By the time he arrived at Sterling's Fortune later that day, he had almost convinced himself that he was going to tell her that. He'd had many long and lonely hours to dwell on her rejection, and he didn't like how it made him feel. Angry, for starters. And foolish.

"I look forward to signing the contract for this deal," Kate said to him. He'd been at the ranch for ten minutes and was so agitated he could barely sit still. He didn't want an earnest conversation with Kate about business. Because his head wasn't up for business when he was consumed by thoughts of Robin and how she'd looked racing from his hotel suite as though her heels were on fire.

"Yes," he said blandly. "I'm sure we'll be able to come to an agreement and let the suits on either side sort through the details."

She nodded. "We can start working on the fragrance immediately. I was speaking with Robin about it only this morning. She's so insightful when it comes to mixing scents and finding just the right balance with plant ingredients. I'd give her a job in the lab in a heartbeat if I believed I could get her out of the garden."

Amersen didn't flinch. He sensed Kate was deliberately provoking him by mentioning Robin. But he wasn't about to get drawn into a conversation about Robin's career goals. "Can I ask where she is?"

"The orchard, I believe," Kate replied, smiling just a little. "If you walk around the rotunda, you'll find it easily enough. Goodbye, Amersen. Thank you for stopping by before you left. It was very unexpected."

He felt about sixteen years old under the older woman's scrutiny. Because Kate Fortune knew exactly why he'd stopped by, and that the reason had nothing to do with their impending deal. But it had everything to do with Robin Harbin.

He said goodbye and left, heading outside. He walked around the gazebo and through an old timber gate and then stepped into the small orchard. He spotted Robin instantly. She was by one of the fruit trees, scraping pieces of bark into a small jar. She wore denim overalls, a long-sleeved red T-shirt, work boots and a purple hat. Her hair was tied up, but that still didn't stop the mental image of her tresses draped over his thighs.

She was so engrossed in her chore that she didn't appear to hear him approach. "Kate said I would find you here."

She jumped and stepped back. "You startled me," she said, scowling. "I was collecting samples."

"So I see."

She placed the jar alongside several others in a carrying case. "The trees aren't fruiting like they've done in the past, and one of the neighboring ranches has had the same problem, so I'm checking for diseases."

Amersen ignored her rambling, because he couldn't have cared less about the trees. He only cared that she was in front of him, within touching distance. He reached out and grasped her hand, rolling out her fingers before placing the unicorn necklace into her palm. "You forgot to take this."

She looked at the trinket. "I didn't forget."

Something uncurled in his gut. A kind of uneasy annoyance that he was unused to. "You don't want it?"

For a moment he was sure he saw her hand tremble. But she then clasped her fingers around the necklace and smiled. "Sure. Of course. It's very pretty and a nice memento of our time together."

Amersen found himself frowning. Something was off. Not right. "Are you angry with me?"

"No," she replied. "Of course not. Why would I be?" She let out a shrill laugh. "It's been a fun week getting to know you, and last night the sex was great."

"Yes," he said quietly, looking for something he couldn't define in her expression. "It was."

She smiled again and met his gaze for just a moment. "So, I guess this is it, then. The final goodbye."

"I guess so."

She picked up the bag beside the tree, shoved the pruning shears into her back pocket and smiled widely. "Okay, take care of yourself, Amersen. Or as they say, *au revoir*!"

He watched as she turned and walked off, hips swinging, shoulders back. No recriminations. No big scene. No asking him when he would call. He should have been relieved. That was how he'd always wanted it in the past. Love them. Leave them. And don't look back.

Now the tables had been well and truly turned. Before he'd had a chance to make some well-practiced speech about timing and it's-not-you platitudes, she'd made the decision for him.

She's done you a favor.

The thing was, he realized as he headed back to the waiting limo and endured the drive to the airport and then the long flight home, it didn't feel like a favor.

It felt like a brush-off.

The first of his life.

Chapter Nine

The thing with taking the high road, Robin discovered as the following week turned into another, was that it could be a lonely place. Really, really lonely. Thank heavens she had her family and her work to keep her mind occupied. Which she did. She played the role of a happy twenty-four-year-old to perfection and fooled everyone.

Except Otis.

The old gardener knew something wasn't quite right with her.

"I guess you're pining after that fancy Frenchman, right?" he asked exactly twelve days after Amersen had flown out of Austin. She hadn't heard from him. She hadn't expected to. But she knew he was back in Paris, back to work and back to his old life. She'd read the blog posts to prove it, including one headlined Single and Loving It! Okay, so perhaps that was not what the post she'd read two days earlier had actually been called, but she hadn't missed the message in it.

And then there was the photo he'd posted on Instagram of himself with a tall, skinny redhead to drive the point home. A picture with some suggestive hashtag that she couldn't bear to read more than a trillion times. A picture that spoke volumes. His arm was around this awful woman's waist. And the redhead, with her pouting lips and slumberous eyes, was leaning close, looking like she'd just had some kind of marathon sex session. A look that Robin knew well, because less than two weeks earlier she'd been the one with the cat-who-got-the-cream expression. And it wasn't the only picture she'd seen. The week before it had been a brunette with exotic green eyes and a flat chest and legs that went on forever. He was everything she'd first believed. A playboy. A man whore. A bed-hopping swine.

And it hurt. So much. So damned much.

Robin laughed at Otis's words, dying inside. "That's ridiculous. Now, we need to talk about the roses that—"

"I got eyes," he said, his craggy face wrinkling. "They might not be good for much, but I still got them. And you haven't been yourself for the past week. I'm figuring it's got something to do with him leaving."

Robin did her best to look hinged and happy. "You're imagining things. I don't get swept up in that kind of nonsense, you know that."

His expression didn't alter. "I know that since that Hammond boy busted you up inside, you haven't been seeing things clearly. But the Frenchman seemed to make things right for you, in here," Otis said and tapped his heart.

Robin stared at Otis, then laughed. "What...are you my love guru now?"

"Someone needs to look out for you," he said solemnly. "Don't you think?"

Although she was touched by his concern, Robin knew she had to change the subject. The last thing she wanted was anyone thinking she was harboring feelings for Amersen Beaudin. With any luck, she'd never see him again. At least she was well and truly out of her dating funk now, and she was grateful to him for that.

Thinking about *anything* else, imagining it was anything else, was simply stupid.

Sex without strings.

Admit it, girl...it was just a breath away from being a one-night stand.

"I'm fine," she assured him. "And to prove it, I have a date tonight."

So maybe calling it a date was a stretch. But she was going out with a few friends for dinner and a movie. Thankfully, it was enough to stop Otis from making any more humiliating observations. When she got home later that afternoon, she showered and dressed in jeans, a bright purple sweater, a scarf and coat, and then headed into town.

She knew she was early the moment she entered Lola May's Homestyle Restaurant, because the place was empty and neither of her friends Mara and Janine was there. But she didn't mind. She waved to the waitress and grabbed a table, sliding into the booth seat as she chucked off her scarf. Then she looked at the scarf and realized it wasn't hers. It was Amersen's. The one he'd draped around her the night they'd watched the movie in the park. She'd almost forgotten she still had it, and certainly she'd had no intention of wearing the damn thing. She fingered the soft wool, felt a sudden and acute sense of loss, and admitted she wasn't fooling anyone by denying the truth of what was in her heart. Even though she knew she'd been right to end things.

"Robin!"

She turned at the excited squeal and saw Francesca Fortune standing beside the booth. Or was it Francesca Fortune Whitfield? She wasn't sure. They weren't exactly close friends, but they had shared a few study groups together at college and were friendly, at the very least. They'd meet up every few months for a quick coffee and catch up.

"Hey, Fran, how are things?"

"Good," the other woman said and sat down with an invitation. Francesca was one of those people who had a bubbly energy around her. With blond curls and brown eyes, she was remarkably pretty and had a broad, infectious Texan twang, much like Robin's own. "Just picking up some takeout. My gorgeous husband loves Lola May's battered fries. Since Friday is our designated date night, we usually eat in, play Scrabble and just hang out together."

It sounded like the perfect way to spend an evening with the person you cared about the most. Robin couldn't help wondering if she'd ever find that kind of someone.

"Didn't you used to work here?"

The other woman nodded. "Yep. Seems like an age ago now. How are things with you? Still working at Sterling's Fortune?"

"Yes. Kate's a great boss."

Francesca's mouth curled, and her eyes widened. "So, is it true that Kate Fortune and that Frenchman Amersen Beaudin are doing business together? I heard he was in town and at the ranch. Did you meet him?"

Robin's stomach rolled. She wasn't about to betray any confidences of either Kate's or Amersen's. As far as she knew, there had been no formal announcement of a business alliance between the two, and she had no intention of speculating. "I did. Although I wasn't privy to their conversations."

"Is he as hot as they say?"

She half shrugged. "He seems very nice."

Francesca laughed. "You're a terrible gossip, Robin—you're like a vault. Which is a shame, because I know Keaton was hoping to speak with him while he was here."

Robin frowned. "He was? Why?"

Francesca's lovely face turned instantly serious. "Oh…it's nothing. Just a business thing, I think. I don't know the details. Anyway," she said as she slid from the booth, "looks like my order is ready. Gotta run. Let's make sure we catch up soon."

Then she was gone, like a whirlwind. Robin remained in the booth, ordered a hot chocolate and drank it, only to be reminded that Amersen had bought her the same the night they'd watched the movie together. Between the scarf and the chocolate, she was suddenly overcome with such hopeless emotion she couldn't stop the heat forming in her throat or the tears burning her eyes. And by the time Mara and Janine arrived, she was crying foolish, wasted tears.

It was Janine who asked the obvious question. "What's going on, Robin?"

She looked up as they slid into the booth. "The worst thing imaginable. I'm in love," she admitted, scratching at her eyes with a Kleenex.

"You are?" Mara said, clearly astonished. "Wow."

Robin sucked in a breath, blew her nose and felt her resolve return. "Yes. And as usual, I've fallen for the wrong guy."

Janine patted her hand. "What do you mean? Did he cheat on you like Trey?"

Robin shook her head. "No…worse. He was honest about everything. He didn't cheat. He didn't lie. He didn't make promises he couldn't keep."

Mara didn't bother to hide her surprise. "Um… Robin, that kind of makes him sound perfect."

"Exactly," she said and sniffed into the tissue. "He's the most perfectly wrong man I have ever met. And I hate him for making me fall in love with him."

Her friends nodded consolingly, as though they understood exactly what she meant.

"So, what are you going to do?" Mara asked.

"Eat chocolate and pretend he doesn't exist," she said, meaning every word, but knowing she had as much chance of forgetting about Amersen Beaudin as she did of going to the moon.

Both were out of the question.

"Is there something going on you would like to talk about?"

Amersen looked up from his desk. At one o'clock on Friday afternoon, the only people who would come into his office uninvited were the nightclub manager, Trudi, his closest friend, Fabien, and his mother. In this instance, it was his mother, Suzette.

"Not now, *Maman*. I am busy."

She ignored him, as he knew she would, came into the room and sat in the chair opposite his desk. "Yes, now."

Amersen sighed, pushed the laptop aside a fraction and looked toward his mother. "Okay, what?"

"You have been back for two weeks and have said very little. I'm concerned."

He ignored the twitch in his gut. He didn't want to have a heart-to-heart with his mother about Texas, the Fortunes or *anything* else. "I told you about Kate's offer. There's little else to tell."

"And…the other thing?"

Resistance crept up his spine. He knew what she was asking. Knew she had her concerns about opening a door to secrets that had been hidden for twenty-five years. "*Maman*, I did not go to Texas to look for my past. It was business."

"Just a coincidence, then?" she inquired "That you go to the same city that is home to your—"

"Those people mean nothing to me," he said quickly. "I didn't speak to them. Or meet them."

"Perhaps you should have."

Amersen stared at her. "Not a good idea."

"I'm not talking about…Gerald," she said, faltering a little over his name. "But Graham and Ben and Kieran and—"

"They mean nothing to me," he said again, cutting through her words as she began rattling off the names of his biological half siblings. "My family is here. You and Papa and Claire. And frankly, I'm sure they have as many reservations about meeting as I do."

She shrugged lightly. "Perhaps, but remember that they contacted you first… That makes their feelings plain enough, don't you think?"

"Keaton Whitfield contacted me first," he reminded her coolly. "And he is another of Gerald Robinson's… mistakes."

Suzette sat back in her seat and stared at him, her gaze softening as the seconds ticked by. "You know, I have never considered you to be a mistake. When I found out I was pregnant, I could only think that you were a blessing. And I still do."

Guilt pitched between his shoulder blades. "*Maman*, I didn't mean to—"

"I did love him," she said, her eyes glittering. "Very much. And I truly believed he cared for me. And despite how things ended between me and Gerald, you *were* conceived in love. Gerald's behavior, once I found out I was pregnant, had nothing to do with you—it was about his own obligations and responsibilities. He was married…something I knew when we began our affair. Children are always the innocents in these things, and the Robinson children are just as blameless as you."

Amersen's instinctive resentment kicked in. "I think they use the name Fortune now," he said evenly.

"That's their prerogative, I suppose. Gerald was Jerome Fortune before he became the man I knew. And blood…blood is hard to deny. They were lovely children—chances are they have grown into good people. People who, despite your reluctance to admit it, *are* your family. And a family that might be worth knowing."

Amersen didn't agree. "You're my mother. Luc Beaudin is my father. Claire is my sister. That's all the family I need. Or want."

"Until you get married and have children of your own, yes?"

He shrugged uncomfortably. "Maybe. One day."

Her mouth curled. "Something you want to tell me?"

"Not a thing," he replied, eager to end the conversation.

His mother clearly wasn't ready to let it go. "You were out of orbit for a whole week—no phone calls, no Instagram, no provocative blog posts. You might want everyone to believe that you were in Texas to see Kate Fortune, but I know you, Amersen…you never fly that low under the radar. Secret business deal or not. If your low profile wasn't about running into your half siblings, then it was something else. And I'm guessing," she said with a grin, "that it has something to do with a girl."

Amersen jumped to his feet as though he had hot coals in his shoes. *Robin.* He was tired of thinking about her. Tired of dreaming about her. Tired of comparing every woman he met to her. He was uncharacteristically confused and didn't understand why he had a knot of rage constantly churning in his gut at the mere idea that she'd brushed him off so easily. He should have been relieved. He should have returned home and gotten back to his life and dated whomever he wanted to and slept with someone else to get the memory of her out of his system. But he didn't. For the first time in his life, he wasn't interested in casual dating. And he was even less inclined to have casual sex.

Because he only wanted Robin.

Getting to know her, spending time with her, kissing her, making love with her. It had all seemed disturbingly surreal. And yet, somehow, the most *real* thing he'd ever experienced.

C'est juste du sexe...

It's just sex.

It couldn't be more. He didn't *do* more. He didn't make promises. He didn't break hearts. He didn't leave a trail of destruction in his wake.

I am not my father...

The acknowledgment exploded in his head like a nuclear bomb.

"Amersen?"

His mother's voice brought him back to earth. "I'm fine, *Maman.*"

She still didn't look convinced. "You're a grown man, and I never tell you how to live your life—even if I sometimes don't approve of your casual approach to things. I'm not going to tell you how to feel about Gerald or your half siblings—or anything else," she added pointedly. "That being said, if you left unfinished business back in Austin, maybe you need to return and either sign on the dotted line or break the deal once and for all."

Later, once his mother had left and Amersen thought about her words. Rife with platitudes, certainly—but she had a point. He wasn't done with Austin. He wasn't done with the Fortunes. And he wasn't done with Robin.

Which meant one thing—he was heading back to Texas.

One Saturday a month, her parents requested that all of the children spend the morning together for a big family breakfast. Robin knew her brothers thought the idea cheesy, but if they were in town, they always complied. It made their mom happy, and if Veronica was happy, Cliff was happy, too. Because when it came right down to it, family was everything.

As rituals went, the Harbin Sunday breakfast was one she'd easily do for the rest of her life. And since it was only a week and a half until Christmas, the family time was acutely special. They had eggs and fried ham, cheese toast and pancakes, freshly squeezed juice and an endless supply of strong coffee. The kitchen was always busy and filled with laughter.

"So," Evan said hesitantly as they set the table with their mother's best china. "Did you hear that Trey got engaged?"

Robin stared at her brother, cutlery in her hands, waiting for pain or rage or despair to settle in her belly and then grip her heart. But…nothing. Zippo. Not a single, solitary feeling. She was, she realized, completely over Trey Hammond.

"How nice for him," she said and laughed heartily. "And awful for her."

Evan looked surprised. "So…you're not upset? You're really okay with it?"

She made a face. "Yes. I just feel a dose of good old-fashioned relief that it's not me."

"That's our girl," Cliff said and grinned. "Gumption by the bucket load."

Robin smiled toward her father. "Thanks, Dad. I love you, too."

"She's getting a prenup," Reece said, grinning. "Or so I heard."

"Smart girl," Robin said and finished with the cutlery. "Speaking of weddings, isn't it time one or both of you got married? Mom and Dad will be wanting grandchildren at some point."

"Count me out for a while," Reece said and grimaced. "One marriage, one divorce. I'm not interested in trying again. At least not for a while." He jabbed a thumb in the direction of Evan. "And no woman in her right mind would put up with Casanova over there. Looks like it's up to you, sis."

Robin laughed loudly. "*Please.* I can think of plenty of things I'd rather do than get married and have a couple of kids."

Liar…

She pushed the wayward thought aside. She was too young to have a biological clock. And too sensible to waste time dreaming about marriage and babies. One day…but not yet. First, she had to find some sweet, eligible man to sweep her off her feet and make her fall madly in love with him.

"There's nothing more rewarding than raising a family," their mother said from behind the counter. "As long as you do it with the right person."

"Oh, no," Evan said and rolled his eyes. "We're going to hear the story about how you and Dad met again, aren't we?"

"It's a good story," Cliff said and winked at his wife. "Very romantic."

"No, please, I beg you," Evan said in mock horror. "Don't say it."

There was an unexpected knock on the front door and Reece quickly moved to answer it so he didn't have to hear the story of their parents' first date and the ensuing first kiss. When he returned a minute or so later, Evan was still pleading with Cliff not to say anything more. Robin looked around and saw Reece hovering in the doorway.

"Uh...Robin...it's for you."

She swiveled on her heels just as Reece moved into the room, and then she swayed back in stunned disbelief.

Amersen!

Her stomach did a stupid, love-starved roll at the mere sight of him. Black trousers, white shirt open at the collar, a black wool jacket that fit him so well she knew it was hand tailored...he looked like he'd stepped off the pages of a fashion magazine. She glanced down at her baggy gray sweatshirt, purple leggings and moccasins and realized how scruffy and unkempt she must look. Well, too bad...it wasn't like she'd been expecting company.

"What are you doing here?" she demanded.

He remained in the doorway and scanned the room. From the corner of her eye, she could see Evan had moved a little closer and her mother had come around the counter. Her father remained seated at the table, and Reece was still hovering close by.

His gaze was blisteringly intense. "I came to see you." He looked toward her mother. "But I see I am interrupting. My apologies, Monsieur and Madame Harbin. I shall come back another time and—"

"There's no need for that," her father said and waved an inviting hand. "Come and sit down, son. Any friend of our daughter's is welcome in our home."

He's not my friend.

She wanted to shout the words at the top of her lungs.

"If you are sure?" he asked politely.

"Of course," her mother said. "You're very welcome."

And suddenly, it was all settled, and now Amersen was sitting opposite her at her parents' kitchen table. No notice. Not a phone call or a text message. She hadn't heard from the man in two weeks *and* he'd been prowling all over Paris, sleeping with every woman he met, but now he was having breakfast with her family as though it was the most normal thing in the world. She'd liked it better when they'd all hated him. Because it was clear that her mother no longer considered him unsuitable and he was back to being all exotic and French and adorable. Even Evan was being civilized, and Reece didn't appear to have an opinion one way or another. But Robin did. She was so mad she was seething inside.

And he knew it.

His blue eyes were glittering, cool and seductive, as though he could read every thought in her head. She could have strangled him. Or at the very least, done some serious damage to his nether regions. Who did he think he was? His arrogance was astounding. How dare he come into her home and seduce everyone with his voice and charm and too-damn-sexy-for-words haircut?

"Are you okay, *ma chérie*?"

His question silenced all other conversation.

She could barely look at him, particularly since she knew her family were all waiting for her response. When she did look up, she glared. *"Ma chérie?"* she echoed incredulously, heat burning her skin as it crawled up her neck. "How dare you call me that."

"Robin, if I have—"

"Who the hell is she, Amersen?" she demanded as she stood and pushed her chair back, tossing her napkin on her plate, ignoring the stunned faces of everyone at the table. "Who's the goddamned redhead?"

Before he could reply, she was away from the table, through the doorway and out of the room. She grabbed a Mexican blanket from the hook by the door and wrapped it over her shoulders as she left the house and kept walking until she was outside and striding toward the corral, heaving in great big breaths, trying desperately not to cry. It wasn't long before she heard the screen door open and close and saw him striding toward her. She raced into the barn and waited, knowing he would follow. When he found her, he stopped a few feet away, hands on hips, feet apart, his eyes bluer than she'd ever seen.

"You need a coat," she said. He'd taken it off inside and hadn't bother putting it back on. She didn't want him catching pneumonia on her conscience. "Idiot."

"Do I get the chance to defend myself?"

"You can't defend the indefensible," she shot back and decided she didn't care if he did catch pneumonia. "Big stupid jerk."

His mouth curled at the edges. "So...the redhead? Care to explain that comment?"

Robin scowled, then fished her cell phone out of

her pocket and within seconds found the incriminating photograph. "*That* redhead!" she spat and held the phone in front of his face. "Looks like you two had quite the night."

He glanced at the picture and then waved a dismissive hand. "I did not sleep with that woman…if that's what you're implying."

"I'm not implying anything," she retorted, fueled by adrenaline and hurt and humiliation. "I'm stating a fact…she's got that look on her face."

"What look?"

Robin wanted to slug him for being so obtuse. "The I've-been-screwing-Amersen-Beaudin-all-night look. I know that look… I've seen it in the mirror."

He took a moment and then laughed. "You're… *jaloux*? Jealous?"

Her humiliation increased tenfold. "I am not."

"Oh, yes, you are," he said, still chuckling. "You are green with it. But it is misplaced, Robin. I do not even know who she is."

"Charming!"

"I mean," he said and took a step closer, "that I cannot recall that photo. It could have been taken some time ago. But it certainly hasn't been taken in the last two weeks."

"How can you be so sure?" she demanded.

"Because this," he said as he stepped toward her and curled a hand around her nape, "this is the closest I have been to another human being in the last agonizing two weeks."

Robin's legs weakened. Oh, he talked a good game. And she wanted to believe him. So much. "But the picture…"

"Forget the picture," he insisted and moved closer. "And tell me why you are jealous."

She melted. "I'm not."

"Shall I tell you why?" he asked, dropping his head a fraction, his intent clear. "It is because you and I...we are not done. You know this. I know this."

He kissed her, and she was lost. Robin clung to him, taking the firm yet soft exploration of his tongue in her mouth as he deepened the kiss. He was so wonderfully familiar. If she'd had any doubts that she had serious feelings for him, they quickly disappeared.

We are not done...

What did that mean?

"You're confusing me," she muttered against his mouth. "Why are you here?"

"I couldn't stay away," he admitted, kissing her again. "Have you missed me?"

"Like a hole in the head," she replied as she took a breath. "God, my family must think I am off my rocker."

"Who is the bigger fool?" he murmured, nuzzling her neck. "The fool who runs, or the fool who follows, hmm?"

"I wish you would go away. I was just starting to forget you."

He pulled back and grasped her chin, raising her eyes to his. "Truly?"

"Truly," she lied. "And don't think just because you're back and looking all sexy that we are simply going to pick up where we left off. First, you haven't really explained what you are doing back in Austin, and second, I'm not sure I want to spend any more time with you."

"Of course you do," he said with so much self-assured arrogance she could only gape at him. "Have dinner with me tonight."

"I can't just drop everything and—"

"Or better still," he said, cutting her off, "spend the day with me. There is still much of Austin that I haven't seen. And I wish to get to know this city of yours a little better. And you."

He wanted to spend time with her. *With her.* She desperately wanted to refuse him. But she was also so deliriously happy to be with him. Like a love-struck fool. Sure, she might end up with a broken heart. But in that moment, the reward outweighed the risk.

"I'll think about it," she said and wrapped the blanket around them both. "First, I have to go back to the house and explain to my family why I behaved like such a fool before."

"Simply blame me for everything," he said and chuckled.

"Oh, I intend to," she said before she dragged his head toward hers and kissed him like crazy.

Chapter Ten

"So, the deal is done?"

They were in Austin later that afternoon, picking up a few gifts for his sister, including a T-shirt that said Keep Austin Weird, since he knew Claire would get a kick out of it.

"With Kate?" He nodded. "Yes. We are in business."

"Congratulations," she said and patted his hand. "I hope it's a huge success. I know Kate wants to start working on the fragrance as soon as possible."

"Yes, I think there will be sample options available within a month. I admit I do not know much about the process of producing a fine fragrance."

"You'll learn," she assured him, and strangely, he took comfort in her words. "I mean, what did you know about owning a winery or a nightclub before you jumped in and gave it a shot?"

"Nothing," he replied. "You are correct."

"You'll find I am right about most things."

Amersen laughed and dropped the parcels on the sofa. He was staying at the same hotel, albeit in a different suite, but it was just as luxurious and well-appointed. They'd been in the room for several minutes, and he figured they were going to end up in bed soon. Their make-out session in the barn earlier that morning had ended abruptly when her nosy brother had come looking for them. They'd returned to the house and spent the next hour with her family. He tolerated their scrutiny, figuring they had every right to ask a few questions. Afterward, he waited while Robin changed, and then they headed into town. They'd had a nice afternoon, one of easy and uncomplicated companionship. And now he wanted to make love to her so much his blood was on fire.

"Come here," he beckoned, holding out his hand.

She stayed where she was on the other side of the sofa. "Oh, no…you don't get me so easily. You're still in the doghouse."

"Doghouse?"

She nodded. "I read your blog," she said, hands on hips. "You know, the one about being single and loving it. The one that said you were painting the town with redheads."

Amersen laughed. God, she was so passionate and vibrant and made him insane and aroused and utterly powerless. "I haven't written a new blog post in weeks. That was something recycled from a couple of months back."

She looked dubious. "Why no new posts? Lost your muse?"

"Lost my mind, more like."

She grinned, clearly delighted, and then she looked a little somber. "I know this is ridiculous… I know we didn't make any promises not to see other people and I know I have no claim on you…but seeing you with that woman made me so mad. And then there was the picture of you with the brunette…"

He frowned. "What brunette?"

She shrugged. "I don't know who she was, just another picture on your Twitter or Facebook."

"I haven't been near another woman since I left Texas," he assured her. "I promise."

She nodded vaguely. "I believe you. Only, it's got me realizing that maybe I'm not the modern-thinking girl I thought I was. Maybe I'm just as insecure and needy as every other person on the planet."

Amersen stared at her, absorbing her beauty and intensity and unwavering honesty. He knew he'd never met a woman like her. She had no agenda—no interest in his money or fame. That was why making love with her had felt so raw and real. And that was why her bailing that morning had wounded so deeply. Because they weren't over. Not by a long shot. He was, he suspected, at the beginning of the first real relationship he'd ever had.

"I really want to make love to you," he said softly.

"I know," she replied, her eyes never leaving his. "I want that, too. But first," she said and waved the shopping bag in her hand, "I want the chance to wear this new dress."

Earlier she'd insisted he wait for her outside a small boho boutique while she looked for a dress. He'd complied easily enough, seeing as he'd be stripping the dress off her at some point.

"Okay," he said agreeably. "I'll take you somewhere for dinner, and then we can come back here and make love all night."

Her brows rose. "All night?"

He shrugged loosely and smiled. "It's been a long two weeks."

She grinned. "What about jet lag?"

"I wouldn't let that stop me."

She laughed and twirled and headed for the bedroom. "I'm going to shower and change."

"I'll book dinner."

"No need," she said as she walked. "I have that covered already."

When she returned to the main suite about half an hour later, his jaw dropped. She looked stunning. The black dress was modest but flared over her hips and made her sensational legs look hotter than Hades, and all he wanted was to see them wrapped around his hips. She had a purple wrap draped around her shoulders and a pair of purple satin shoes on her feet.

"*Mon Dieu*, you look beautiful."

"Thank you. Now, go and get dressed and we can get going."

He chuckled and headed for the bedroom, showering and changing his clothes quicker than usual because he didn't want to miss any more time in her company than he had to. Once they were on the road, she gave him directions and he drove a few miles out of the city.

"You haven't said where we're going," he said as he took a left turn and headed west out of town.

"It's a surprise."

Amersen looked at a roadside sign. "The Hill Country?"

"It's a nice spot," she explained. "Better in the daylight, but I know you're just going to adore where we're going. It will take about half an hour, but it's worth the drive, I promise you."

The excitement in her voice was contagious. *Mon Dieu*, he loved that about her...

Loved...

He almost brought the vehicle to a screeching halt as the word banged around in his head.

I do not love this woman...

I can't...

It was just desire. Mind-blowing, off-the-charts, out-of-this-world sex that was unlike any he'd experienced before. But still, *only* sex. Heat, sweat and release. Nothing more. He had the pattern set. Three dates, get laid, a last date, send flowers and then adieu.

But just thinking about his usual pattern made him feel sick to his stomach. Was that who he had become? A man with such little regard for the most intimate thing two people could do together, a man who treated women like playthings? Sure, he'd never played roulette with birth control or ever said *I love you*, but did that really make him any different from the one person he never wanted to be compared to? *Gerald Robinson*. Was being an honest and indifferent asshole toward women any better than lying and deception?

No...

"Are you okay, Amersen?"

His whole body tightened. "Fine," he denied, for a crazy, guilty moment wanting to turn around and take her home to her ranch.

"Good," she said, and he could hear her smile. "Next right, turn."

He did as she asked and spotted a sign that said Mendoza Winery. He'd heard anecdotally about the place but knew little of its history. Amersen followed the road, turned into a driveway and drove beneath a tall set of open gates.

"It's amazing in the daylight," she said as she reached over and placed her hand on his thigh. Her touch was light but possessive, and he didn't mind one bit. "The vines run on either side, and there are several really amazing gardens here and the most brilliant sculpture garden out the back. You just have to see it."

"Is that why you like it so much? For the gardens and the sculptures, not the wine?"

She chuckled. "You know me, always thinking about what I can plant where."

"Kate said she would offer you a job at Fortune Cosmetics in the laboratory if she thought you would accept."

She sighed lightly. "I know. But I'm happier outside."

Five minutes later they were inside the restaurant and seated at a table she had booked. The place was high-end and well-appointed, and he thought that adding the restaurant and function rooms to the winery was a solid idea. Not something he'd want to do at his own place, but it clearly appeared to be a successful venture. Their table was discreet and well positioned, overlooking the gardens. Several heat lamps had been fired up to add warmth and atmosphere, and the place was humming. Waitstaff hovered, taking their drink order, and when the wine they ordered arrived, it was a heady merlot he liked very much. The Texas wine industry was a growing concern, not as steeped in tradition as places like Napa, but the reputation of the wines was growing accordingly. Even as a competitor, Amersen could appreciate a quality product.

"How does it measure up?" she asked, as though reading his thoughts. "I mean, to yours."

He chuckled softly. "That's something of a loaded question, *ma chérie*."

She smiled, her blue eyes glittering with the promise of what the night would hold. The truth was, he couldn't wait to strip off her sexy dress and make love to every inch of her. He wanted to feel her beneath him, he wanted to watch her come apart in his arms, he wanted to hear his name on her sighs as she convulsed with pleasure.

"I like how you call me that," she said and watched him over the rim of her glass.

He tapped his chest lightly. "It is what is in here. Perhaps I say it better in my native language than English, yes?"

Before she could respond, a waiter arrived and they ordered their meals. When the man left, the intimate mood had shifted slightly, and she talked about Christmas and asked him questions about Paris and how long he would be staying in Austin.

"I am…unsure. However, my business with Kate will no doubt bring me back here in the future."

"Good."

Amersen saw doubt in her gaze and reached across the table and grasped her hand. "I don't want to mislead you, Robin. That is not who I am."

"I know," she said and squeezed his fingers tightly. "I guess I would like to see where this might lead."

His gut took a dive. Because he wanted that, too, and the fact they lived in different countries was a glaring, insurmountable obstacle. He wasn't sure it was something they could get past. And yet he suddenly had an image of her beside him, hands linked as they walked through his vineyard on the hill.

Their meals arrived shortly afterward, and he watched as she savored every mouthful of the stuffed chicken breast. Everything with Robin seemed like an adventure. Eating good food, sipping wine, walking through the streets of Austin, watching an old movie, making love as though there was no tomorrow.

"Excuse me, you're Amersen Beaudin, correct?"

He turned at the sound of a deep male voice to his left. A man in his early thirties stood near their table, dressed in a dark suit. Amersen didn't know him, but he was used to being recognized. Of course, it mostly happened in his hometown, but the world was a much smaller place thanks to social media. Amersen placed his wineglass on the table and nodded. "Yes, that's correct."

The man held out his hand. "Good evening. My name is Alejandro Mendoza. Welcome to the Mendoza Winery."

Right. So he'd been recognized, because this man was obviously the owner and knew he also owned a vineyard and produced wine. He shook his hand and quickly introduced Robin. She smiled and said hello, and then he turned as much attention as he could muster to the other man. "It's a pleasure to meet you."

"Likewise. I hear you have the best winemaker in the entire Loire Valley. It must be challenging trying to keep him at your vineyard."

Amersen smiled to himself thinking that the humble yet passionate seventy-year-old winemaker Jean-Pierre would laugh out loud if he knew he was being discussed as the best in the business from the other side of the globe. "It is what many say. Although he has already turned down three job offers this month. But if you feel you can match the ridiculously large salary I pay him, please, take a shot."

Alejandro laughed. "Well, you can't blame me for trying. Oh, I'd like to introduce you to my wife."

"Of course."

"Querida," Alejandro said and beckoned someone to his side. Within seconds an attractive, slender woman with long dark hair and brown eyes sidled up

beside the other man. "Liv, I'd like you to meet Amersen Beaudin... Amersen, this is my wife, Olivia Fortune Mendoza."

Amersen's skin turned bitingly cold, and he angled his head and met the woman's gaze. He saw the shock in her expression and then the quick way she masked her surprise. There was no doubting it.

She knew.

He felt his lungs tighten, experienced a familiar dread crawling across his skin as he jerked his gaze away. He could hear Alejandro Mendoza jabbering on about how he owned a vineyard and was a celebrity and was known by his first name on social media, but the sound of his voice became a drone in Amersen's ears. All he heard was one thing.

Fortune.

This woman, with her haunted brown eyes, was a Fortune. One of *the* Fortunes.

She smiled tentatively, muttered something to her husband and quickly excused herself. As she walked off, Amersen experienced an intense surge of relief. Except for the tightness in his chest and the feeling that he could barely a drag a breath into his lungs. Alejandro lingered for a moment, offered Amersen a return visit during the day to inspect the vineyard and wished them a pleasant evening. Once the other man was gone, he took a breath, and then another, the tightness increasing, the discomfort rising in his chest. Amersen knew where he was heading, knew his lungs would fail him if he didn't do something about it.

"Are you okay?"

Robin. It was the first time she'd spoken in minutes. He met her gaze and saw concern and confusion in her expression. "Actually…no. I don't feel well. Do you mind if we finish here and head out?"

The furrow about her nose increased. "No…of course not."

Once they were back in the car, Amersen grabbed the inhaler he'd tossed into the glove compartment earlier that day. The thought of Robin witnessing him struggling for breath was unbearable…but if he didn't use the inhaler, he knew he would be in for a full-blown attack. He took a puff. And then another, not daring to look in her direction.

Finally, she spoke. "Are you okay?"

He glanced sideways, seeing her concern and hating that she'd witnessed him needing his medication. "Fine," he lied, his pride well and truly battered.

"What happened in there?"

Amersen shrugged. "Nothing. Just a combination of cold night air and jet lag. I told you I was an asthmatic."

He didn't want to lie to her…but he wasn't in any mood to come clean, either.

She didn't look convinced. "Let me drive back."

"No," he said, harsher than he liked. "I'm fine."

"Amersen, please let me—"

"I don't need to be coddled, Robin. The inhaler did its job and I am back to normal. Stop fretting."

She opened her mouth to speak again, but Amersen gently placed a finger to her lips.

"I assure you, I am quite fine now. Please don't worry."

Her eyes glittered. "Okay."

He managed to control his breathing as he drove her back to her ranch, knowing she would say something when she realized they weren't headed to his hotel in the city.

"Oh...I thought..."

"I have some international calls I have to make to-night," he said, trying to keep his voice as light and unaffected as possible. Trying not to let her see that he was coming apart at the seams. "Sorry, Robin, I should have said something earlier."

"Oh, well...okay. I understand."

But he knew she didn't. She would be hurt and confused and rightly so. But he couldn't say anything else. It was too much. Too hard. Too...close to her potentially seeing him in pieces.

"I'll drop your things by tomorrow, if that's okay?" he suggested when he pulled up outside her small house.

She nodded, her hand on the door handle. Then she stilled. "Amersen...have I done something to—"

"No," he said quickly and grabbed her other hand, raising her knuckles to his mouth. "I genuinely don't feel well and don't think I will be any kind of company tonight. I will make it up to you, okay?"

She nodded a little but didn't look convinced. "Okay."

Amersen got out and walked her to the door, kissed her softly and then left before he changed his mind. He waited until she was inside and the door was closed before he headed back to the car. He took a slow, deep breath, and then another, trying to focus, trying not to think about Robin, or the fact he wouldn't be making love to her that night, since he'd cut their evening short. Because he couldn't think of anything other than the one truth that was churning through his blood.

That barely an hour earlier, he'd come face-to-face with Olivia Fortune Mendoza.

His sister.

Robin woke up Monday morning with a head full of conflicting emotions. Including anger and a whole load of confusion. What had started out as a romantic, wonderful day had ended so abruptly she was trying to work out what had gone so disastrously wrong.

It didn't make sense. Amersen had pursued her. He'd flown back to Texas, he'd arrived at her family home and endured the scrutiny of her parents and brothers. He'd insisted they spend the day together. And the night. They'd flirted and touched and she'd believed they would make love. But…no. Because instead of the dreamy, passion-filled night she'd anticipated, he'd dropped her off at her doorstep with little more than a perfunctory kiss and then bidden her good-night with some vague indication that he'd see her soon.

Hot and then cold.

As though something had happened to change his mind about them. Which made her replay the entire day and evening over and over in her head. And every time she got to the point where Alejandro introduced his wife to them, Robin came up with the same answer. Amersen had shut down the moment he came face-to-face with Olivia Fortune Mendoza.

Because he knew her. It was the only possible reason. He knew her and didn't want anyone to know it. Including Robin and Alejandro. Olivia was a beautiful woman. A beautiful *married* woman. And both Olivia and Amersen had looked like they wanted to be somewhere else the moment Alejandro made the introduction.

She felt sick to her stomach the moment she suspected it. It couldn't possibly be true, could it?

Amersen had insisted he knew no one in Austin. Every possible scenario raced through her head as she got dressed in jeans and a sweater and pulled on her purple boots. Did they know each other from some old acquaintance? Was it a new relationship? Was it serious? Was it intimate?

She spent the whole day making herself crazy with possible scenarios. And ignored the call and two text messages he sent her around lunchtime. Because what she had to say to him, she wanted to say face-to-face.

She left work early, and by the time she drove to his hotel, it was close to three o'clock and she sent him a text message as she strode across the foyer.

We need to talk.

Her cell dinged barely seconds later.

I know. I'll come to your place.

She replied immediately.

No need. I'm downstairs. Meet me at the elevator.

A couple of minutes later, he met her by the elevator door. He didn't say a word. Neither did she. He simply grasped her elbow and led her into the elevator, and they traveled up to the top floor in silence. Once they were in his suite, he poured her a glass of wine, grabbed the one he'd obviously been drinking—since it was half-full—and sat down on the sofa.

She took a good look at him and realized he looked tired and as though he had some great burden pressing down on his shoulders. He hadn't shaved, so dark stubble shadowed his jaw, and his clothes were crumpled. They looked like the same clothes he'd worn the night before. He wasn't looking at her. He had his elbows on his knees and was staring into his wineglass. Something, she realized, was seriously wrong.

Robin decided there was little point in playing games or stalling simply because she didn't want to face the truth. So, she jumped right in.

"Are you sleeping with Olivia Fortune Mendoza?"

That made him look up. And right into her gaze. His mouth was a harsh, thin line.

"Don't be ridiculous."

Robin winced. "Then what?" she demanded.

He shrugged and looked away. Clearly, it wasn't a conversation he wanted to have. Well, too bad.

"Oh, no," she said and moved around the coffee table. "This isn't where you get to be all moody and closed off. Because if you don't answer the question, Amersen, I will walk out the door and we'll never see one another again."

His gaze rose instantly. "I can't..." His voice was ragged and uneven, and he placed the wineglass on the table with an unsteady hand. "I don't know what to tell you."

"The truth," she said, gentler this time, because she saw a kind of raw vulnerability in his expression that she'd never seen before. "I just want the truth."

He took a long breath, sounding as though it was one of the hardest of his life. "Olivia is... She's my..."

She'd never seen him struggle for words as he did now. And when he spoke again, his blue eyes were glittering bright and were filled with uneasy emotion.

"She's my sister."

Sister?

Robin absorbed his words, trying to make sense of them and failing. It didn't make sense. Amersen's sister was called Claire and she lived in Paris. And Olivia was

a Fortune who'd married a Mendoza. What possible link
could there be between her and Amersen? Robin tried
to connect the dots in her head and failed, coming up
with more questions instead of answers. She remembered what he'd told her about his parents and that Luc
wasn't his biological father. And then the penny suddenly dropped in spectacular fashion.

*Oh my god…*could it be true? Could Amersen Beaudin be one of the illegitimate Fortunes?

"But…but that would mean…that would mean that
Gerald Robinson is your—"

"Nothing!" He got to his feet and paced around the
sofa, hands clenched, arms at his sides, his shoulders
tighter than she'd ever seen them. "He's nothing to me.
Just the man who got my mother pregnant."

She heard the pain and resentment in his voice, and
her heart ached for him. "Who knows?"

"No one," he replied flatly. "Just my parents. And
Keaton Whitfield and Ben Fortune. And Olivia, by her
reaction last night." He ran a weary hand through his
hair. "And probably the rest of the damned Fortunes."

"Kate?" she asked quietly.

He shrugged. "I'm not sure. She's never mentioned
it—but I have no idea if that's why she invited me to
Austin, or whether it really was about the business deal.
All I know is that seeing Olivia last night made me
think I should reconsider this whole cologne idea."

"Why?" she asked.

"Because I'm not sure I want anything to do with
anyone named Fortune," he replied harshly. "You saw
the look on Olivia's face… She was no more impressed
by the meeting than I was."

"She was probably surprised," Robin suggested, trying to act impartial—which was hard when he looked

so achingly vulnerable. She'd never seen him lacking confidence like he did in that moment. "But, despite that…you are related. Once the shock wears off, you might be able to get to know her…and the rest of them."

"I'm not sure I want to."

"But they do, right?" she inquired as she placed her wine on the side table and moved around the sofa. "They've offered the olive branch, haven't they? Or at least someone has? Keaton?"

He frowned instantly. "How did you know that?"

"I bumped into his wife, Francesca, on Friday," she explained and then gave a brief account of the conversation. "So, he obviously wants to make contact. What's holding you back?"

He looked at her incredulously. "Are you serious?"

"Perfectly."

He shook his head with a kind of impatient disdain. "How about the fact that I've been ignored for the last twenty-five years?"

"Well, I think the family only discovered that your…" She paused and found some different words. "That Gerald had other children a year or so ago. And with Keaton arriving in town and falling for Francesca and then Chloe being acknowledged as a sibling and her marrying Chance, I guess there's been a lot going on for everyone."

"Yes," he said with a scorn she'd never heard before. "I'm sure it's been unbearable for the legitimate children of Gerald Robinson discovering they have so many other *bastard* siblings around the globe."

Robin felt his pain so much her insides hurt. "What are you afraid of, Amersen?"

"Afraid?" he scoffed. "I'm not afraid of anything."

But she knew he was. She reached out and grasped

his hand, holding it tightly within her own. He didn't pull away. He didn't move. He looked at her, meeting her gaze with a kind of burning intensity that drew her toward him like a moth to a flame. She wanted to help make things right for him.

"I wish you'd told me."

"Why?" he shot back. "So I could see that pitying look on your face a whole lot sooner? No, thanks."

"Because we're friends," she said quietly. "And friends help one another."

He looked down into her upturned face, and the mood quickly shifted. "I don't want to be friends with you," he said and bent his head, all vulnerability gone, replaced by a burning look of awareness and sexual longing so intense it curled her toes. "I want to make love to you."

She knew what he wanted—to exorcise his demons with sex. And she should have pulled back and put space between them. But she couldn't. She loved him. He was hurting. And she would do whatever she could to help ease the pain in his heart and soul.

"Then make love to me," she said and pressed closer. "And let me make love to you."

He looked at her for a moment, as though making some monumental decision, and then he kissed her, long and hard and deep and, in a way, a little angry. But she matched his kiss and his touch, and when they finally made it to the bedroom and started stripping off clothes, his hands were caressing her so exquisitely she was all out of coherent thought. He touched her between her legs, and when he found her wet and ready, he made an almost agonized sound low in his throat. Once he had birth control in place, she accepted him eagerly, holding his hips firmly, and he moved inside her, finding an erotic, wild rhythm that made her climax almost immediately. There were no words, nothing other than the need for pure sexual release between them. It felt divine. It felt like she was being driven higher and higher with every pulsing stroke. And it made her a little sad, too. Because she knew in that moment that it was all she could give him. She loved him and gave herself up, holding him tightly as his orgasm brought him shuddering against her.

Afterward, he rolled off and disappeared into the bathroom. When he returned, he sat on the edge of the bed. She knew he didn't want to speak and didn't want her advice or counsel. But he was going to get it, regardless.

"I think you should talk to Olivia."

"No."

Robin sighed and placed her hand on his bare back. "If you're feeling like this, then chances are she is, too. What have you got to lose?"

He didn't move. "My edge."

Ah—pride. She wanted to hug him and slap him at the same time. "Maybe it's the person with the stronger character who takes the most risk."

He shrugged off her touch and walked to the window, naked and unselfconscious. The curtains were open, but the tinted windows gave complete privacy. He stared out of the window for a moment and then spoke.

"You should go home. I'm not in the mood for company."

Robin hurt right through to her soul. But she knew he was hurting, too. And she wanted to help him. Because…because she loved Amersen Beaudin with every part of her heart. She loved his brash confidence and his self-assured belief that he was right about every single thing. She loved that he was romantic and gave her silly gifts that meant so much. She loved that his kisses made her head spin. She loved the way he looked directly into her eyes when they made love. And she loved that she was seeing him raw and vulnerable and he couldn't hide it from her, no matter how much he tried.

She knew he was fighting his feelings. And a part of her was, too. She'd never been in any kind of hurry to settle down into a relationship. Even being with Trey had simply happened without any real effort. And she knew Amersen hadn't been thinking of anything long-term when they met a few weeks ago. But, looking at him, seeing him so hurt and conflicted about who he was, made her realize that she was deeply invested in him. *In them.* A part of her knew she was wishing for the moon…and that he needed to work out his feelings toward the Fortunes before they could even contemplate taking their relationship any further forward.

He had to face who he was.

And suddenly, she knew exactly what she needed to do.

Chapter Eleven

Amersen picked up his cell phone at least half a dozen times the following morning before he summoned the courage to call Robin and apologize for his appalling behavior the night before. He'd asked her to leave, and she had. Without hysterics or recriminations or complaint. And he felt like the biggest heel of all time, because he knew he'd hurt her. He didn't have to see the wounded look in her eyes as she'd dressed. He'd used her to get all thoughts of the Fortunes out of his mind—and it felt wrong.

She answered on the third ring. "Hello, Amersen."

The fact she recognized his number made him feel worse. She knew him. Because somehow, in a matter of weeks, that was what they had become. An item. A couple. *A relationship.* The idea rocked him through to the very blood in his bones. He remembered what his mother had advised before he'd returned to Texas, some platitude about signing on or breaking it off. The truth was, he didn't know what to do. The thought of not seeing Robin again caused a physical ache in his chest. But if they continued as they were—disaster. He wasn't stupid; he knew what he saw in her eyes when they were together. And he…he had so many conflicting feelings churning through his head and his heart, he didn't know what the hell to do.

"I'm sorry about last night."

She sucked in a short breath. "Okay."

"I was…angry," he explained, an inexplicable heat burning his eyes. "Not with you. With myself. With the whole…*situation*."

"I understand."

"Are you sure?" he asked.

"Of course."

"Can I make it up to you?"

"Sure."

Her staccato responses unnerved him, and he hated that she could do that. He didn't feel anything like his usual self when he was around Robin. His overconfidence had often been described as arrogance and cockiness, and he'd never bothered to waste time altering those opinions. It was good for business, and in the past, business was all that mattered. But not anymore. Robin had an uncanny ability to strip down his defenses.

"Shall I pick you up so we can spend the rest of the day together?"

"I'm working. But perhaps we could meet later." She hesitated for a moment and then asked a question. "How long are you staying in town?"

"I'm not sure," he said and then realized she would be looking for assurances. "Perhaps a few days. It is Christmas soon and I need to get home to my…to everything there."

"Okay," she said after a moment. "I'll come to the hotel after lunch. I need to pick up my things that I left there. Give me a couple of hours."

When she hung up, Amersen felt uneasy and couldn't define why. She hadn't sounded right. Not angry, which was what he'd expected. Not confused, which he'd figured she was probably feeling. But agreeable. Too agreeable. Which meant one thing. She was ending it.

Good. It saved him the bother. She could come to his hotel, collect her things, maybe they'd spend the night together in one final goodbye. They could have hot, mind-blowing sex, and then they would be done. If that was what she wanted, he'd accommodate her.

It was after twelve when he was alerted by the concierge that she was on her way up. And barely a couple of minutes later he heard a sharp tap on the door. He pulled the door back, and as soon as he saw her, every ounce of blood in his veins heated. She wore jeans, a soft purple sweater, a scarf, boots and a jacket, and her beautiful hair was loose. His heart skipped a crazy beat. And then every thought he had about ending things with her disappeared. He didn't want to end things. He wanted to start things. He wanted to haul her into his arms and kiss her beautiful mouth and do it every day for the rest of his life.

"What took you so long?" he said, dying to drag her to bed for the rest of the day. "Come in."

She hesitated, her gaze shifting to the right. Amersen peered around the door and froze.

"Hello, Amersen."

Olivia Fortune Mendoza was at his door. He immediately glared at Robin, seeing assurance in her expression as rage percolated quickly in his gut and then churned throughout his entire body.

"What is this?" he demanded.

Robin squared her shoulders and walked past him, inviting the other woman into the suite.

By the time he was in the lounge area, both women were seated on the sofa. Robin looked pensive. Olivia looked nervous. And Amersen was so angry he could barely get his legs to move.

"I called Olivia and asked her to come here because I thought the two of you should talk."

It was Robin's voice, but he hardly heard it above the rage gathering momentum and screeching through his ears every time he took a breath. "You did." He scratched the words out and knew he sounded like he was chewing sandpaper. "Did you?"

She looked at him, her blue eyes unwavering. "You need closure. You need to sort this out."

Annoyance and resentment settled in his blood. "I don't think it's anyone's position to tell me what I need."

"I think you're wrong," she said quietly, unmoving. "I think sometimes, when someone is hurting, it's up to the people who care about that person the most to make sure they do right by them. And that's what I'm doing."

"What you're doing," he seethed, not daring to look at Olivia, his rage all directed toward Robin, "is interfering in my life. And assuming that you have the right. Which you do not."

"But I thought—"

"You thought wrong," he said harshly. "I wouldn't accept this kind of interference from even my closest friends, let alone someone I hardly know."

As soon as he said the words, he saw her recoil. But he was pissed off and couldn't control his words at that point.

He looked toward Olivia. "My apologies, Mrs. Fortune Mendoza, for your wasted trip. I'm sure Robin will see you out."

He strode off and headed for the bedroom, slamming the door to make the point that the conversation was over. *When* he was ready to face any of his half siblings, it would be his decision. And he'd make sure Robin understood she wasn't to interfere in his life. He heard the suite door open and close and took a couple of puffs of his inhaler before he stalked back out into the main room. He was stunned to see that Robin was no longer there. But Olivia Fortune Robinson—now Mendoza— was sitting exactly where she had been when he left the room, knees crossed, hands in her lap.

She looked up and raised both brows. "Have you finished sulking?"

He stilled instantly. "Where is—"

"She left," Olivia supplied, head at a tilt. "Not that I blame her. You really are as stubborn and pigheaded as we've all come to believe."

It was a pretty mild insult, and he'd had far worse over the years, but it still irritated the hell out of him. "We?"

She waved an impatient hand. "Oh, come on. We both know that Keaton and Ben have tried to contact you and that you have ignored every request. And you've been back and forth to Austin twice in the last few weeks and still didn't make contact with any of us. Shame on you."

Shame on him? He almost laughed out loud. "I hardly think that it is my—"

"Are you so self-absorbed that you think you are the only one suffering here?" she demanded, sitting upright on the sofa. "Do you have any idea how it feels to discover that there's a dossier on the results of your father's indiscretions? And to discover that the father you've believed in all your life is someone else entirely? Someone who has children with other women, someone who is now painted as some kind of ogre?"

He rocked back a little on his feet. She had a valid point. He'd never spared much consideration to the feelings of Gerald Robinson's children. His jaw suddenly felt like it was carved from granite. "I guess I don't."

"Some of us don't want to play the victim card, Amersen," she said pointedly. "Some of us are willing to try to work through this. He made mistakes—big ones—but who hasn't made mistakes in their life?"

Amersen ignored the tightness in his chest. He'd never considered himself to be a victim. And he didn't like the label one bit. "He ignored my existence for twenty-five years. He ignores me still. That's not a mistake. That's a choice."

Her mouth thinned. "God, you're so much like him—so arrogant and self-important."

He didn't ever want to be compared to the other man, and was about to tell her so, when Olivia spoke again.

"He didn't know about you," she said and sighed heavily. "Look, I wasn't going to bring this up because it's obviously something you need to sort out with your mother…but all I know is that she told my father that she'd ended her pregnancy, and as far as he knew, that was the truth."

"He paid her off," Amersen said quietly, refusing anyone to lay any blame at Suzette's feet. His mother had told him the truth—Gerald never wanted the child she carried. *Never wanted him.* Suzette made the choice to have Amersen on her own, and he was grateful for that decision. He was also thankful that Luc Beaudin had entered her life. "And he was relieved when he believed she had *taken care* of things."

Olivia shrugged. "I guess it was a difficult time for them both. All I'm saying is that he didn't ignore you… he didn't *know* about you. It was *my* mother who knew," she explained, and he could see how much the truth hurt her. "She knew about the dossier and kept the information to herself. She knew about you and Keaton and Chloe and the others that are in it. It's not a pretty story, okay? My mother has played her own part in this situation and she, along with the rest of us, have to live with that. And yes, our father has known about you for a while now and hasn't made contact, but can you blame him? He knows he's not going to get a good reception from you—is he? It's not like you have this great reputation for being all warm and fuzzy."

"I don't think my reputation should matter," he said tightly.

"Of course it does," she said and waved an impatient hand. "We all know who you are. What you are. That you have this opinionated and cynical skew on life. I've read your blog and your bio, Amersen. You're not perfect. And he's not perfect, either. But he's trying to make amends in his own way with Keaton and Chloe. If you give him a chance, he'd probably try to do the same with you."

"Probably?"

She sighed. "Like I said, he's not perfect."

Amersen's head reeled. Everything Olivia had just told him about Gerald and Charlotte made the whole sordid mess somehow less sordid. And then, without warning, part of the weight that had been pressing down on his shoulders since he'd first discovered he was Gerald Robinson's son slowly lifted.

For months, he'd made a point of denying any biological link to the other man. In his core, he believed that Gerald was a dishonest, womanizing cheat who betrayed everyone he got close to—and Amersen never wanted to be that kind of man. So, the farther he withdrew, the less chance he had of ever being compared to the one man he had grown to hate above all others. Even before he knew of his biological father's identity, he knew enough about the quality of man he was—married and unable to remain faithful. A consummate liar. A man who promised everything and delivered nothing. A man who left a trail of emotional destruction in his wake. That was why Amersen never let himself feel anything other than desire in his relationships and why they were brief and ended before he was in too deep. No investment—no possibility of leaving that same trail of destruction and pain. Absolute proof that he was *nothing* like the man who had given him life. And the knowledge that no one would be hurt. Including him. *Especially* him.

The realization made him laugh to himself. For so long he had kept people at a distance. He had success and wealth and fame and everything he'd ever dreamed of. Except the one thing that really mattered…complete and utter emotional surrender to another human being.

Until Robin.

"You look like you've just had some kind of revelation," Olivia said quietly, and he saw that she was smiling.

It occurred to Amersen that he liked her. His sister. His blood. "I think I just did."

Her mouth twisted slightly. "Well, maybe it's not me you should be admitting that to?"

He let out a long and weary breath. "She left me."

"Because you were a stupid jerk," Olivia said and smiled. "You know, don't be offended when I say this—but you really are a lot like him. You're both driven and innovative, and you both clearly attract women like flies to honey. But," she said when he went to protest, "that doesn't mean you have to *be* him. All I'm saying is, learn from his mistakes. You know, when Robin called the vineyard this morning and asked me to come here to speak with you, she knew you would be angry. But she did it anyway. That should tell you all you need to know."

"She shouldn't have—"

"People do stupid things when they're in love," Olivia said and laughed. "Just ask my husband."

"Robin doesn't—"

Olivia waved her hands, cutting him off. "You know, for a smart guy, you're pretty stupid."

Amersen had taken all the insults he was prepared to take from his half sister. "She's not in love with me."

Just saying the words hurt him through to his bones.

"Of course she is," Olivia said quickly. "Otherwise, she wouldn't have called me. What did she have to lose? Only everything," Olivia said, answering her own question. "If that's not love, I don't know what is. And you're in love with her…only you're too stubborn and proud to admit it."

His head reeled.

"I'm not in love with her."

"Sure you are," Olivia said and laughed. "Now go and tell her that."

Amersen's feet felt as though they were stuck in cement. He didn't want to admit anything his sister was saying to him was the truth—that he was stubborn, that he was foolish, that he was anything like Gerald Robinson…or that he was in love with Robin.

But denying it would have been the biggest lie of his life.

"I will tell her," he said and grabbed his keys. "But there's something I have to do first."

It was time he faced his father.

* * *

Robin believed she knew what a broken heart felt like. But nothing had prepared her for this.

Not even an hour spent with Butterfly could soothe the ache in her soul that reached right down to her bones.

Someone I hardly know...

That was what he'd reduced their relationship to. Nothing. She hurt so much she was all out of tears. Everything had turned out exactly as she'd suspected it would from the beginning. The coldness in Amersen's expression spoke volumes. The man had ice in his veins. He didn't deserve any tears *or* her broken heart.

"Mom called."

She turned her head and spotted Evan standing by the doorway. "And you raced over here?"

He shrugged. "She said you broke up with the Frenchman."

"Would you stop calling him that?" she snapped and tossed some hay into Butterfly's stall. "And to be broken up, we would have had to be *together*...which we weren't," she added pointedly.

Evan grinned. "Yeah, right. The guy means nothing to you."

"That's not what I said," she said hotly. "However, whatever we had, it's over."

Evan came a little closer. "Mom said he's Gerald Robinson's son...is she right? One of the secret Fortunes?"

Robin nodded fractionally. Even though she'd decided she would hate Amersen until the end of time, talking about his private business felt like a betrayal. "I shouldn't have told Mom," Robin said and sighed. "We all know she can't keep a secret."

"But I can," Evan promised and looked solemn. "I'm a lawyer—lots of practice. So, what happened?"

Robin figured there was little point in keeping it to herself and gave her brother an abridged version of events over the last couple of days—leaving out the part about how she'd slept with Amersen and he'd told her to leave—and then how he'd dismissed her so cruelly in front of Olivia Mendoza.

"Well, you can't blame the guy for being a bit messed up," Evan said when she finished.

Her gaze narrowed. "You're taking his side?"

"I'm on your side," he assured her. "But it would be a hell of a shock to come face-to-face with a secret sibling, particularly in a public place while you're on a romantic date. And you did kind of interfere by inviting her to his hotel."

Trust Evan to be the voice of reason. "You sound like a lawyer. I was trying to help. When you care about someone, that's what you do."

"You're not thinking about this the way a guy would."

Robin stared at her brother. "What the hell is that supposed to mean?"

He sighed. "It's like you getting mad at me and Reece because we didn't tell you about Trey cheating. We genuinely didn't tell you because we didn't want to hurt you. But you think we kept it from you because we wanted to control you or something when we just wanted to protect our sister. And you made Amersen confront something that he probably wasn't ready to because you're a woman and you don't have a problem facing your feelings. But guys...not all of us are comfortable doing that. It's in our DNA to *not* want to talk about how we feel. It makes us uncomfortable and vulnerable. That's probably how he felt when you forced his hand. And when he got mad, you were hurt, and there's the cycle all over again."

Robin rocked back on her heels. "Is that really how men feel?"

"Yep. Most of the men I know, anyway."

"You poor things," she said drily. "I guess I have a lot to learn."

"Stand in line," he said and laughed softly.

Robin met his gaze and her throat constricted. Sometimes Evan was a jerk, but sometimes he was the best brother in the world. "Thanks. I needed a pep talk today."

He hauled her into his arms and gave her a bear hug. "And for the record, I'm sorry Reece and I didn't tell you about Trey. I promise that it was only because we didn't want to see you get hurt. Can you forgive us?"

"Of course," she said and sighed.

"And don't be so hard on yourself. Or your Frenchman. I mean, if you love the guy…"

"Right now I hate him," she said and sniffed as hot tears plumped at the corners of her eyes.

Evan laughed and hugged her close. "Same thing, sis…same thing."

The Robinson estate was big and intimidating. Typical of a family home when the family in question wanted for nothing. The gardens were decorated with festive lights and Amersen figured he'd find much of the same inside. He arrived at the front security gate, gave his name and was admitted instantly. He waited in his car for a few moments before he got out of the car, headed up the pathway, tapped on the front door and waited. Foolish, he supposed, to simply turn up unannounced. Particularly since he might run into Charlotte. The last thing he wanted was to cause anyone any distress. But he had to do this before he lost his nerve.

The door opened and a tall, solid-looking man who clearly took care of himself stood at the threshold. He had gray hair and dark eyes that were riveting and impossible to shake.

My father.

"Hello, I'm—"

"I know who you are," Gerald Robinson said and stepped back. "I heard you give your name to the house-keeper."

A thousand emotions raced through Amersen's entire body. He wasn't sure how to feel. Angry. Resentful. Edgy. He'd imagined the moment countless times and had prepared himself to be filled with enough rage to start a war. But what he truly felt was an all-consuming sense of relief.

And then the older man held out his hand. Amersen wavered for a moment, unsure, feeling about sixteen years old…imagining he was that boy again, the one who demanded to know who he was and then saw the pain in his mother's eyes when he learned the truth. A pain that this man—*this sperm donor*—was responsible for. So he waited for the familiar rage to manifest itself. But it didn't come. And then, without really knowing how, he reached out and shook Gerald Robinson's hand.

"Come inside," Gerald said when Amersen pulled his hand free. "We should talk."

The home was as impressive inside as out. As expected, it was decorated within an inch of its life with Christmas elements, which reminded him of Robin's little house—and then the thought of her sent his stomach plummeting.

Once they were seated in the large living room, Gerald spoke again.

"It took a lot of guts for you to come here."

Amersen didn't flinch. "I figured one of us had to be the first to face the other."

Gerald nodded. "You're right. It's been a long time coming. I suppose you have a lot of questions."

Amersen's chest constricted, and he forced air into his lungs. *Not now.* He took a second and thought of wide-open spaces. He thought of water. He thought of air. And he thought of Robin. And then his lungs were free. *Thank you,* ma chérie.

He took a breath and looked at Gerald. "I have one question. Why do you cheat on your wife?"

To his credit, the other man didn't shrink back from his query. "Because for better or worse, women have always been my biggest weakness. And I find them hard to resist."

"Every woman you meet?" he shot back, unflinching.

"That is a slight exaggeration," Gerald replied. "But I can see why you might think that…considering."

"Considering I'm sitting here, you mean."

Gerald's mouth twisted in a brief half smile. "You have your mother's eyes."

Amersen tried not to let the mention of Suzette's name change the tempo of the conversation. He didn't want to start a fight. He didn't want to hear stories about twenty-five-year-old broken promises. But he did want the truth.

"I know what transpired between you and my mother when she worked for you. It's not a road I wish to go down with you. But I would like to know this—you have been aware of my existence for some time. Why have you not made contact?"

Gerald met his gaze, took a long breath and sat back in the chair. "I didn't think you needed me to. You appear to be in control of your life… I didn't want to interfere with that."

It was quite the admission, but Amersen wasn't quite ready to let the other man off the hook. "How could you interfere? I don't know you."

Gerald looked at him. "You know me, Amersen. You know me when you look in the mirror. You knew me when you made your first million. You knew me when you bought that vineyard and planned to produce the best wine in the region. You knew me when you decided to come to Austin to talk with Kate Fortune. You know me every time you have an idea or plan some risky business transaction." He leaned forward. "Because I'm in your blood."

Amersen stared at him, and as he did, the resistance and rage he'd been harboring for months suddenly faded. Not completely, but enough for him to really see the man who sat in front of him.

Flawed. Earnest. Scared.

Everything that he was, too. And he knew, in that moment, that he had a choice. He could be a coward and tell Gerald Robinson to go straight to hell and forget the man existed. Or he could accept who and what he was. Luc Beaudin would *always* be his father. But perhaps, with time and patience and compromise, this man could be something, too. He wasn't sure what…perhaps a mentor or friend. But he was willing to at least leave a window of opportunity open. He was man enough to admit that he could. And that he wanted to.

"I'm tired of being resentful toward you," he admitted.

"Good," Gerald said flatly. "Resentment is a wasted emotion. And it's certainly wasted on me."

Amersen nodded. "I have good parents. A solid family. I'm not looking for another. I don't want anything from you, either," he stated, laying it out. "I don't want or need your money, your name or your success."

"I know that," Gerald said and nodded. "You have that all on your own. Despite how it might seem, I'm actually very proud of you."

Amersen made a self-deriding sound. His father was proud of him? Ironic, since he wasn't particularly proud of himself right now. "I've tried really hard to *not* be like you."

"And how's that working out for you?"

"It's not," he admitted and then said a brief goodbye to the older man."

"Will I see you again?"

Amersen shrugged lightly. "Maybe."

Gerald nodded. "Thank you. That's more than I expected. Maybe more than I deserve."

Amersen left the room and insisted on seeing himself out. He was out the front door and three steps down the pathway when he met another man coming in the other direction.

Ben Fortune Robinson.

His brother.

It took about two seconds for the other man to recognize him and another few seconds to realize he was shaking Ben's hand.

"About time you showed up," Ben said and grinned. "Olivia called me, she said you were coming to see the old man, so I thought I would drop by for some moral support."

Amersen's back straightened. "For me, or him?"

"For whoever needed it," Ben replied. "Did you get the answers you wanted?"

"Some," he admitted.

"Well, that's a start, I guess. The thing is, he hurts people without trying…you might say it's in his nature."

"That doesn't let him off the hook."

"No," Ben said agreeably. "But when you really think about things, I guess most of us are guilty of hurting the people or person we love most at some point…don't you think?"

Amersen scowled. "Your point?"

"The Harbin girl," Ben said matter-of-factly. "Olivia said you screwed up big-time."

Amersen actually laughed. "Privacy is clearly not a big thing in your family."

"Your family, too," Ben reminded him. "So, you screwed up. Not the first time. Won't be the last. The question is, what are you going to do about it? Are you going to be a fool and let her slip through your fingers?"

"I hadn't planned on it."

"Then what did you plan?" Ben asked. "Is she a fling? Or is she the marrying kind?"

Marriage…

Amersen's already knotted stomach was doing back-flips. "Ah…yes…that kind."

Ben offered a broad grin. "Then take some advice— go and get a ring and do the right thing."

Amersen laughed loudly. If someone had told him a couple of weeks earlier that he would be standing outside his biological father's house having a civil conversation about engagement rings with his half brother, he would have dismissed the notion entirely.

But by five o'clock he was driving toward Robin's home with a ring in his pocket.

And hope in his heart.

Chapter Twelve

Robin was just coming out of the bedroom after taking a shower when she heard a knock on her front door. She glanced down at her gray sweats and purple moccasins and figured she looked decent enough for company. She half expected it to be her mother or Evan, who was staying with their folks for dinner, or even her dad coming to check on her. They had all spoken to her at some point over the course of the afternoon. She was grateful for their love and support, but she really just wanted to be miserable in private.

But it wasn't her family at her door.

It was a ridiculously huge bouquet of flowers, followed by the last person she'd expected to see. Especially since she spent most of the afternoon convinced that they were over and done with.

"What do you want?" she demanded when Amersen's handsome face came into view from behind the flowers.

He held out the bouquet. "To apologize."

His eyes were glittering so blue she could barely look into them. "Go away."

He smiled. "I can't."

She looked at the bouquet and grimaced. "I can't be bought off, Amersen. I told you that...gifts don't cut it with me."

"Then what?" he asked, still standing beneath the doorway. "What do you need? What do you want?"

She pressed a hand to her heart. "I want this. I want what is in here."

He swallowed hard. "You have it. Unconditionally."

Robin's heart leaped through her chest. How she wanted to believe him. But how could she? He'd made his feelings about their relationship abundantly clear just hours earlier.

"I don't believe you."

"Let me in," he said, his silky voice like a caress down her spine. "And I will prove it to you."

Oh, right. Sex. That was what he wanted. That was why he was at her door. A quick roll between the sheets before he flew back to Paris.

"If you want a quickie, then go find a redhead," she said, hurting through to her bones. "I'm sure you'll find one in town. I'm tired of being your latest fling."

He laughed. "I only want a particular blonde," he said, then turned somber. "And I'm glad you don't want a fling. Neither do I. Please, Robin…let me in so we can talk."

"I don't want to talk to you. Go back to your hotel."

"You're being stubborn and unreasonable."

Unreasonable!

She stepped back and slammed the door in his face. Then she stalked up and down the hall, cursing him under her breath. Hating him with every fiber in her body. He knocked again. And again. And again. In fact, he knocked eight times. And when he gave up and headed back down the steps, she muttered to herself how it was typical, since he gave up so easily. She peered through the curtain, expecting him to head for his car. But he didn't. He was walking toward her parents' house.

What's he up to?

He looked so good, too. In his black pants, black shirt and dark coat, everything about him screamed elegant style. The best money could buy. Well, he couldn't buy her.

She squinted to see what he was up to, scowling when she saw the back door of her parents' house open and Amersen ushered inside. Robin's insides churned. Damn.

She grabbed her phone and texted her brother.

What's going on?

A couple of minutes later, her cell pinged.

Your boyfriend's here.

She scowled again and pressed buttons like a crazy person.

He's not my boyfriend!

Evan's next response was quicker.

Sure looks like it from here.

She stared at the text, ignored his teasing and then replied.

What's going on in there? What's happening?

It took the longest thirty seconds of her life for her brother to respond.

He's talking to Dad. Sounds serious.

Robin's breath caught in her throat. Amersen was talking with her father and it sounded serious? It didn't make sense. What would he possibly have to say to her dad?

What are they talking about?

Her brother responded within seconds.

You, I'm guessing.

She wanted to race up to the house and demand to know what was going on. Except that a minute later she saw the back door of her parents' house open and then spotted Amersen striding in her direction.

By the time Amersen had trudged back to Robin's door, she was standing on the porch, looking hopping mad. He still had the flowers in his hand and the stupidest grin on his face.

"Are you out of your mind?" she demanded when he reached the bottom step.

He looked up and shrugged. *"Peut-être…possibly."*

She clamped her hands to her hips. "Did you actually just talk to my father about me?"

He glanced back toward the main house, saw her brother, mother and father standing by the back door and then smiled. "News travels fast around here."

She scowled. "What did you say to him?"

"I asked for his permission to marry you."

Robin's heart almost stopped. "What?"

He shrugged loosely. "It seemed like the right thing to do. To show that I...that I respect you and your family. And to show you that you have changed me."

Her head reeled. "You're insane. Give me one good reason why I should marry you."

"Because it's Christmas soon, and it will be the worst one of my life if you say no. But, mostly, because you love me?" he suggested hopefully, placing one foot on the bottom step. "Or because I love you."

She looked like she wanted to throw something at him. "Love me? You love me now? You didn't appear to love me this afternoon when you said we hardly knew one another."

"I was angry," he said quickly. "I said something stupid and insensitive and I am sorry."

She still didn't look convinced. "But you were right. We don't know one another very well. And now, out of the blue, you turn up on my doorstep and start talking about marriage? It's...it's...crazy thinking."

"I'm crazy for you, Robin," he admitted and came up the steps and pushed the flowers into her hands. "That is all I know." He reached into his pocket and was about to get down on his knee when she grabbed his arm and kept him upright, obviously conscious that her parents and brother were still watching them from across the yard.

"Oh, no," she said and dropped the flowers on the love seat by the door. "I don't want any more gifts from you. Particularly one that goes right here," she said and held up her left hand.

Amersen's insides crumpled. "You are refusing me?"

"I'm saying that—"

"You are all that I want," he admitted, feeling her getting further and further out of his reach. It hadn't occurred to him that she might refuse his proposal, and then he realized how arrogant that made him sound. The thing was, he was pretty sure she loved him. No—he was *certain* that she did. "Do you not love me?"

She dropped her hand and stepped back. "That's not the point."

"Then explain, please?"

She pointed to the flowers and to his pocket. "The point is, flowers and diamonds are not who I am. The fact you keep giving them to me shows you don't know me at all."

"Then tell me," he implored. "Tell me what you want."

"I want you to know me," she said and held a hand to her chest. "I want you to know me deeply, in here. I want you to know what I like, what I fear, what I dream about. And I want to know you. Not the image you portray to the world—sexy and charming and brash—but everything else. Like what you dream about, what name you want to give the first child you have, what makes you happy and what makes you cry. The real you," she said, her voice breaking, and he saw the tears in her eyes. "That's what I want."

Amersen wanted to hold her so much his arms actually shook. What she was asking for was something he'd never given to anyone before. And it terrified him.

"I...I...I've never..."

"I know," she said when his words trailed off. "That's why it's so important. Without it, we can't be anything."

He backed up slowly and headed down the stairs, striding toward his car. When he reached the vehicle, he saw Robin on the porch, shaking her head slightly before she retreated inside. He grabbed a few things from the car and then headed back to the house. This time he didn't knock. He walked straight inside. It was time to take what he wanted.

She was in the living room, seated on the chintz chair by the fireplace. The room was exactly as he'd remembered. Pure Robin. The lights on the Christmas tree already sparkled. The glass slippers he'd gifted her were still on the mantel, alongside the snow globe. She didn't want gifts. She wanted him.

Every ounce of love he had in his heart felt like it was suddenly on his sleeve.

But she still looked skeptical.

"I know you wear purple because it was your grandmother's favorite color," he said quietly. "You never talk about her, but I know she was important to you because there are several photographs of her in your parents' home, with you at her side. She used to make hats for you, purple ones, and you are wearing one in the picture above the fireplace. I know that being outside in a garden makes you happy and feeds your soul. I know that you want to visit many cities around the world but have not been able to afford to. I know that you want to find a relationship as loving as the one your parents have. I know that the cowboy you used to date made you feel as though you were lacking in some way. But be assured, *ma chérie*, you are not." His gaze never left hers, and he saw the tears glittering brightly in her eyes. "I know that you say chocolate is your favorite food, and you actually like mint-flavored chocolate the most. I know that you feel free and alive when you are out riding your horse. I know that one day you hope to have a home with a garden so big you could spend all day walking around the grounds. I know you are kind and considerate and have sweetness etched into the deepest parts of your soul. It is why I have fallen in love with you."

She was crying, and he longed to haul her against him. But he wasn't done. He pulled a few items from the bag in his hand and placed them on the coffee table.

"This is my inhaler," he explained, his throat tight. "When I was a child, I spent much time in the hospital, and after many rounds of medication the doctors recommended I start swimming, which I did, and the health of my lungs improved. You've seen me use it, and I admit I felt a little uncomfortable..." His words trailed off and he swallowed hard. "No, that is not right. The truth is, I felt *vulnerable*...and that is something I am not used to feeling with anyone. I don't like feeling that way with anyone. But with you...it is different. I don't mind it as much. I feel safer."

Robin wiped another tear away as Amersen continued. "And that," he said, pointing to a dog-eared little book, "is my English/French dictionary that my father gave me many years ago, when I was still in school. I take it everywhere with me because sometimes I forget the right word when I am speaking English, even though I have an app on my phone that will do the same thing. And this," he said, motioning toward a battered leather key ring, "is the first thing I bought when I made my first paycheck when I was sixteen. And if I am ever fortunate enough to be blessed with children, I would like to call our first daughter Sarah."

She didn't blink at the way he said *our*. But he couldn't deny what was in his heart. He hoped one day to be a father—to share a child with Robin. He hoped he would be as good a parent as his own. He also hoped he could earn her love and keep it for all the days of his life.

"I know I have many flaws. I know I do not always play by the rules. But I always trust my instincts." He took a breath—long and hard and shuddering. "And my instincts are telling me that this is right...that I am exactly where I want to be. You asked me what I dream. That is simple, *ma chérie*, my dreams...my dreams are all about you."

He finished speaking and swallowed the heavy lump of emotion in his throat. She hadn't moved. But tears were streaming down her face. Amersen blinked and realized he had tears in his own eyes, and he stepped forward, aching all over, his hands trembling. He knew what she wanted—he knew she would never settle for half measures with him. With them. She wanted all that he was, every fault, every fear, every vulnerability that he'd always carried like a burden, determined to be a better man than his biological father.

He held out his hands toward her. "My hands are full with money and ambition and fame...but without you, Robin, they are empty. You asked what makes me cry. That is easy to answer—imagining my life without you in it."

He waited as she got to her feet. Waited as she took a couple of steps toward him. Waited as she wiped the tears from her cheeks and then pressed her thumb to the corner of his eye, feeling the moisture there. Then she pulled back and spoke, arms folded, eyes wide. "Are you quite finished?"

"Yes," he said, his voice raw. "I have nothing else."

"Then stop talking and kiss me."

There was invitation in her expression, and he needed no other encouragement. Within seconds she was in his arms and he found her lips with his own, quickly losing all coherent thought as he kissed her beautiful mouth. He thrust his tongue inside, groaning as she pushed against him.

"Do not toy with me, Robin," he said raggedly against her lips. "Tell me what I want to hear. Please."

But she didn't respond with words. She grabbed his head and anchored him to her, kissing him with a kind of hunger that undid him. He returned each kiss, touching her through her clothes, which suddenly wasn't enough. Her hands were on his chest, his shoulders, and she was tugging at his jacket. He quickly ditched the jacket and her impatient fingers began unbuttoning his shirt and pulled it from his waistband. And they kissed—long and deep, drugging kisses that were hot and wet and fueled by the hours since they'd last touched. Amersen ran his hands down her back and settled on her hips for a moment before he grasped the edge of her sweatshirt and pulled it up. Within seconds the rest of their clothes were gone, landing in places around the room, and they were on the rug in front of the Christmas tree, naked, chest to breast, legs entwined, mouths fused together as their kisses got hotter and deeper.

And finally he was inside her, staring down into her beautiful face. She had never looked more lovely than she did in that moment. *"Je t'aime, ma chère,"* he whispered against her mouth and then translated. "I love you, my darling."

She sighed and wrapped her legs around him, holding him close. "I love you, too. So very much."

Amersen's heart almost exploded in his chest. "Thank you," he said and buried his face in her neck, moving inside her, feeling her tremble and shake beneath him. In that moment, nothing else existed—just Robin, just her legs and her arms and her sweet mouth. Just the sensuous, loving delirium that rocked him through to the core. The dim memory of other faces, other bodies, faded, and in his heart and soul there was now only her. Just this one woman he loved so much. "Thank you for loving me in return."

She gripped him hard, and they came apart together. It was more than pleasure, more than sheer release, more than anything he'd experienced before. It was as though they had risen up and found the moon, the stars, the sun and every other planet in the universe.

When they returned to earth, he didn't move. He couldn't. His legs were heavy, and his arms were going numb. But he didn't care. He just wanted to hold her for eternity.

"You know," she said softly, kissing his shoulder. "We have to move at some point."

"I cannot bear the thought of being apart from you."

"I'm not going anywhere," she assured him. "But I am a little cold right now."

She had a point. By now it was dark outside, and they'd neglected to start a fire. But he didn't want to ruin the mood by worrying about a fire.

He moved and sat up, grabbing a blanket from the back of the sofa and wrapping it around his shoulders, before he settled himself against the wall and then cradled her in his lap, her back pressed against his chest. "So, you never did answer the question."

She turned her head, resting her cheek against his collarbone. "Actually, I don't think you asked. More like demanded."

He knew she was teasing, and any other time he would have played along, but not having an answer was killing him. "Marry me? Please?"

She grabbed his hand and linked their fingers intimately, smiling audaciously. "So...where's my ring?"

He grinned. "In my jacket."

"Where's your jacket?"

Amersen pointed across the room. "Over there."

She giggled and stretched, grabbing a fire poker while trying to keep the blanket over her nakedness. Then she used the poker to fish for his jacket and dragged it along the carpet, laughing delightedly.

"You know," he said after several attempts, "it would probably be easier to walk over there and get it."

"But nowhere near as much fun."

"True," he said and trailed a series of kisses across her nape. "But try not to put a hole in my jacket, okay, *ma chérie*?"

She laughed, clearly finding him hilarious. "You are such a slave to fashion, city boy. I suppose I also need to get used to your handsome face being plastered on every billboard in Texas once Amersen Noir is launched," she said as she tossed the jacket at his face and then laughed again.

Amersen growled playfully and then extracted the small velvet box from the pocket. He held it in front of her and waited. It took about two seconds for Robin to take the box and flip the lid.

"Oh." She sighed. "It's beautiful. Simply perfect."

The purple amethyst, set in platinum, was surrounded by a series of flawless diamonds—as soon as he'd spotted the ring, he knew it was the one for Robin. The delight in her expression was all the confirmation he needed on that score.

"Does that mean you'll wear it?" he asked hopefully.

She held the ring between two fingers and looked at him. "How long have you had it?"

"About three hours," he replied. "Ben helped me choose it."

Her nose wrinkled. "Ben?"

He grinned ruefully. "My...half brother."

Her blue eyes widened dramatically, and she turned in his arms. "What? You saw him?"

"Saw him," he said. "Met him. Talked with him. And I talked to Gerald."

Her expression softened. "And how did it go?"

He shrugged one shoulder. "Better than I had imagined. I'm not saying it's going to be easy, but it was... okay."

She reached up and touched his jaw, pressing her palm lovingly. "I'm so proud of you."

Heat pricked his eyes again, and he laughed at himself, wondering when he'd become such an emotional fool. "So, are you going to marry me?"

She looked deeply into his eyes, and a lovely smile curled her mouth. "Yes, I am."

Robin could barely contain the happiness that was surging through her heart. The beautiful ring was now in place on her finger, and Amersen was kissing her with such sensual expertise she was deliriously breathless and happy.

"When?" he demanded against her mouth.

She considered a sensible approach. "We'll have a two-year engagement."

He shook his head. "No...impossible. Too long."

"Twelve months," she amended, threading her fingers through his hair. "I'm not going to be rushed, and you're not going to always get your own way with me. You have a lot going on and we need time to get to know one another. Twelve months," she said again. "No compromise."

He half smiled. "Okay. Unless you get pregnant,"

he said, his eyes smoldering. "And since we just made love without protection, those particular cards may be on the table."

Pregnant?

She was dizzy thinking about having Amersen's baby. And she wanted it. Maybe not yet, but one day.

"Tell me what happened with Gerald," she prompted, curious and eager to shift the subject a little.

He sighed heavily. "I knew I had to face him…otherwise I would never have been able to get on with being who I am. In my heart, I am Luc Beaudin's son, but I also know I cannot ignore everything else. I can't pretend that the Fortunes don't exist…particularly since I am going into business with some of them. And you know, perhaps that's why this deal appealed to me," he admitted quietly. "Perhaps, in some way, this is how I take small steps toward them. All I know is that I had to take ownership of whose blood is in my veins. Before I could offer you anything, I needed to face that part of myself."

She looked at him solemnly, loving him with every part of her heart and soul. "So, do you forgive me for the whole thing with Olivia?"

"Do I forgive you for interfering in my life and making me face my demons?" He touched her chin gently. "Yes. Do you forgive me for hurting you and making you feel as though you…*we*…didn't matter to me?"

She nodded. "You were angry, I understand."

He gave a self-effacing grimace. "I was scared. I knew you could see right through me. All my life I have done exactly what I wanted. The money and fame, I am ashamed to say it came easily. Not that I didn't have to work hard, but the results were there straight away, and I have lived a selfish life since. I got away with treating women poorly because I have notoriety and money, and that behavior does not sit well with me now. Because of you," he said, running his thumb across her lips. "Because you challenged me and fought me and called me out when I behaved badly. I need that. I need you. I need you to always make me want to be a better kind of man."

"You're the best man I have ever met," she assured him.

He smiled. "That is nice to hear, but probably not exactly true. But I promise I will be the best man I can be, for you. I will be the best husband I can be, and the best father I can be to our children."

Robin's heart soared. "You really want kids?"

"Absolutely," he replied. "One day. But first, there are many things I want to do with you. I want to take you to Paris and show you my little vineyard on the hill. And every Christmas I want to take you to a different city so you can realize your dreams."

It sounded like heaven. But it was all happening so fast she could barely draw a breath. "You know, we've only known one another for three weeks...this is so unexpected it's making my head spin."

"Does time really matter?" he asked softly. "I knew I loved you the first moment I saw you."

Robin stared at him in openmouthed shock. "You did?"

He nodded. "You were walking through the garden at Kate's ranch. I could not see your face, but you were wearing that white dress and that crazy big hat and you looked as though someone had plucked you from one of my dreams. My heart felt as though it had stopped. I did not understand at the time... I thought it was mere attraction and that it would fade. I thought that kissing you and making love with you would erase my desire for you—that it would make me behave as I always did." He held her chin, looking reverently into her eyes. "But it did not. It simply made me love you more. My feelings will never fade, Robin. *Je t'aime*. I love you."

Tears welled in her eyes. "I love you so very much, Amersen. And I can't wait to see your house on the hill. Which does pose a sticky question…where are we going to live?"

He pulled her close and the blanket fell, and she knew they should have been cold…but they weren't. "As long as we are together, does it matter where we are?"

He had a point, she thought as she kissed him.

All that mattered was that they were together. For the rest of their lives.

Epilogue

Robin picked up that something was wrong the moment Amersen answered the phone.

"What is it?" she asked when he ended the call.

In was Christmas Eve, and they were picking up the remainder of Amersen's things from the hotel suite before they headed to Paris on a late-night flight. They had spent a wonderful afternoon celebrating Christmas with her family, and although she was sad that she wouldn't be spending Christmas Day with them as usual, she was super excited about heading to Paris to meet her future in-laws and his sister, Claire. She had a belly full of jitters, but she knew Amersen would be close at hand to help her through her nerves.

"That was Kate," he explained and came around the sofa. "We have been summoned to Sterling's Fortune."

"Summoned?"

"Our company has been requested."

Robin glanced at her watch. "But won't we miss our flight?"

"Kate has arranged for us to fly home on her private jet," he said as though it was nothing out of the ordinary. "And there's a limo waiting downstairs."

And just like that, half an hour later they were pulling up outside the ranch house at Sterling's Fortune.

"I think I could seriously get used to this rich-and-famous thing," she said and took the hand he offered as they got out of the limo. "Maybe we should think about getting our own jet."

He laughed, and the sound made her giddy with love for him. The last week had been filled with love and passion and a kind of surreal happiness. They had spent every possible moment together, and their connection was stronger than she could have ever imagined.

"There are a lot of cars here," he said, more seriously.

Robin's eyes scanned the parking area, and she spotted several fancy cars and SUVs. She was so busy looking around, she didn't notice that Amersen had stopped walking.

"Are you okay?" she asked and reached for his hand.

"I'm not sure I'm ready for this."

She knew what he meant. The past week they had spent in a kind of hazy couple bubble, not letting anyone intrude on their time together. She knew he had deliberately steered clear of the Fortune family, and she'd respected his need to take things slowly.

Robin squeezed his hand. "I'm here," she said and urged him toward the house. "I'm right here with you."

He kissed her and whispered soft words against her mouth. "I know. That's the only reason I am not racing back to the car right now." He lifted his head and took a breath. "Let's get this done."

If Amersen had any preconceived ideas about what it would be like meeting the rest of his half siblings en masse, he threw them out the window the moment he stepped into the main living room. With Kate as hostess, he had no option but to face them all in one swoop. The names whirled around in his head in a jumble—

Ben and his wife, Ella; Keaton and his wife, Francesca; Graham and his wife, Sasha, and their two young daughters; Kieran and his wife, Dana, and their little girl; and so many others he whispered to Robin that she would have to remember half of the room for him. Olivia came forward first, breaking the ice by giving him a brief hug and making the first few moments marginally less awkward than they could have been.

"Are you annoyed with me for doing this?"

Kate Fortune's voice made him turn. Resplendent in an ivory silk suit, she was smiling as she passed him a champagne flute. They had been mingling for about ten minutes, and he was glad for the reprieve while Robin took a moment to speak with her friend Francesca and show off her engagement ring, much to the delighted squeals of the other woman.

"I wasn't sure you knew," he said and took the glass. "You never said anything."

"I rarely show my entire hand," she replied. "But I wanted to assure you that this had nothing to do with my reasons for our business venture." She smiled a little. "Well, mostly." She looked around the room and sighed. "They are good people...all of them worth knowing. As are you."

"Thank you, Kate."

She moved off just as Keaton and Ben approached. Amersen searched for Robin out of the corner of his eye and mentally willed her to return to his side. It took about thirty seconds for him to spot her weaving a path toward him.

"You know, we're not so bad," Ben said and laughed. "Just ask Keaton... This time last year, he wasn't sure he wanted to know us, either. And look how good it turned out," he said and slapped the other man on the shoulder in a kind of brotherly affection Amersen had never been a part of.

Brothers...

These are my brothers.

As he glanced around the room, he could see the familial resemblance, and by the time he stopped looking, Robin was back by his side. She discreetly grasped his hand and held it tight.

"It's good of Kate and Sterling to play hosts tonight," Keaton said and nodded.

"Yeah," Olivia said as she came up between the two men. "It would be a bit awkward doing this at the ranch, with Mom being there."

Ben groaned. "Oh, this is Olivia, by the way—she's the sibling who always says what's on her mind."

Amersen's mouth twitched in a smile. "We've met. She gave me a roasting."

"You deserved it," Olivia said and glanced at Robin. "But I'm glad to see you took my advice."

He grinned. "Me, too."

"It's hard at first," Keaton said more seriously. "But it's worth it, in the end."

"And you're always welcome to be a part of things," Olivia chimed in. "Now we need to find the others so we can all get to know one another and act like a real family. So make sure you stay in touch."

"I will," he assured her. "We will. And since I'm going to be living in Austin for the next six months, I'm sure we'll have time to get to know one another."

It had been an easy decision. He needed to be close to work on Amersen Noir with Kate, and there was no way he was going to pluck Robin from her home and family and career and plant her in Paris without any compromise.

"And after that?" Olivia queried.

"After that, we'll see," Robin replied, squeezing his hand. "I like the idea of living in Paris for six months of the year. Whatever we do," she said and laughed so delightfully his heart physically ached, "it sure won't be boring."

Everyone agreed. And then Keaton made a toast.

"To family," he said as glasses were raised. "Old and new. Here or not. And to making new memories. Merry Christmas!"

Amersen raised his glass and leaned toward Robin. "*Joyeux Noël*, Robin. This will be the first of many wonderful holidays together."

She reached up and kissed him, and his family cheered.

His family

And then he swept her up in his arms and held her close, thinking that for the first time in his life, he really did have it all.

* * * * *

Looking for more Fortunes? They'll return next month in the new Special Edition continuity

THE FORTUNES OF TEXAS: THE RULEBREAKERS

Nathan Fortune left the navy and returned to Paseo, Texas, vowing to put the past behind him. Until Bianca Shaw and her son show up on his doorstep and Nate finds that the past won't stay buried...

Don't miss

HER SOLDIER OF FORTUNE
by
Michelle Major

Available January 2018, wherever Harlequin books and ebooks are sold.

***

And catch up with

THE FORTUNES OF TEXAS: THE SECRET FORTUNES

Look for:

A FORTUNE IN WAITING
by Michelle Major

HER SWEETEST FORTUNE
by USA TODAY *bestselling author Stella Bagwell*

FORTUNE'S SECOND-CHANCE COWBOY
by USA TODAY *bestselling author Marie Ferrarella*

FROM FORTUNE TO FAMILY MAN
by USA TODAY *bestselling author Judy Duarte*

FORTUNE'S SURPRISE ENGAGEMENT
by Nancy Robards Thompson

WILD WEST FORTUNE
by New York Times *bestselling author Allison Leigh*

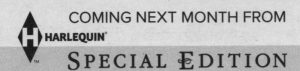

Get 2 Free Books,

Plus 2 Free Gifts—

just for trying the Reader Service!

SPECIAL EXCERPT FROM

H HARLEQUIN®

SPECIAL EDITION

*When his best friend's little sister shows up with her son,
Nathan Fortune's past won't stay buried…and threatens
to snuff out the future Nate and Bianca now hope to
build with each other.*

*Read on for a sneak preview of
HER SOLDIER OF FORTUNE,
the first book in the newest Fortunes continuity,*
**THE FORTUNES OF TEXAS:
THE RULEBREAKERS**.

"He's an idiot," Nate offered automatically.

One side of her mouth kicked up. "You sound like Eddie. He never liked Brett, even when we were first dating. He said he wasn't good enough for me."

"Obviously that's true." Nate took a step closer but stopped himself before he reached for her. Bianca didn't belong to him, and he had no claim on her. But one morning with EJ and he already felt a connection to the boy. A connection he also wanted to explore with the beautiful woman in front of him. "Any man who would walk away from you needs to have his—" He paused, feeling the unfamiliar sensation of color rising to his face. His mother had certainly raised him better than to swear in front of a lady, yet the thought of Bianca being hurt by her ex made his blood boil. "He needs a swift kick in the pants."

"Agreed," she said with a bright smile. A smile that

made him weak in the knees. He wanted to give her a reason to smile like that every day. "I'm better off without him, but it still makes me sad for EJ. I do my best, but it's hard with only the two of us. There are so many things we've had to sacrifice." She wrapped her arms around her waist and turned to gaze out of the barn, as if she couldn't bear to make eye contact with Nate any longer. "Sometimes I wish I could give him more."

"You're enough," he said, reaching out a hand to brush away the lone tear that tracked down her cheek. "Don't doubt for one second that you're enough."

As he'd imagined, her skin felt like velvet under his callused fingertip. Her eyes drifted shut and she tipped up her face, as if she craved his touch as much as he wanted to give it to her.

He wanted more from this woman—this moment— than he'd dreamed possible. A loose strand of hair brushed the back of his hand, sending shivers across his skin.

She glanced at him from beneath her lashes, but there was no hesitation in her gaze. Her liquid brown eyes held only invitation, and his entire world narrowed to the thought of kissing Bianca.

"I finished with the hay, Mommy," EJ called from behind him.

Don't miss
HER SOLDIER OF FORTUNE by Michelle Major,
available January 2018 wherever
Harlequin® Special Edition books and ebooks are sold.

www.Harlequin.com

THE WORLD IS BETTER WITH

Romance

Harlequin has everything from contemporary, passionate and heartwarming to suspenseful and inspirational stories.

Whatever your mood, we have a romance just for you!

Connect with us to find your next great read, special offers and more.

f /HarlequinBooks

🐦 @HarlequinBooks

www.HarlequinBlog.com

www.Harlequin.com/Newsletters

A *Romance* FOR EVERY MOOD™

www.Harlequin.com